P9-DKF-749

# CITY

## OF

# WIDOWS

## Other works by Loren D. Estleman

# CITY

## ⁓ OF ⁓

# WIDOWS

## LOREN D. ESTLEMAN

**FORGE**

A TOM DOHERTY ASSOCIATES BOOK

NEW YORK

This is a work of fiction. All the characters and events portrayed in this book are fictitious, and any resemblance to real people or events is purely coincidental.

CITY OF WIDOWS

Copyright © 1994 by Loren D. Estleman

All rights reserved, including the right to reproduce this book, or portions thereof, in any form.

This book is printed on acid-free paper.

A Forge Book
Published by Tom Doherty Associates, Inc.
175 Fifth Avenue
New York, N.Y. 10010

Design by Lynn Newmark

ISBN 0-312-85667-9

First edition: April 1994

Printed in the United States of America

0 9 8 7 6 5 4 3 2 1

For Debi, *mi arma y mi salvación.*

"These widows, sir, are the most perverse creatures in the world."
—Joseph Addison (1712)

"Be wery careful o' vidders all your life."
—Charles Dickens (1837)

# CITY

## OF

# WIDOWS

# ఇా 1 ఇా

GENERAL LEW WALLACE had a grip that could crack corn and no chin at all under a beard that was like a fistful of nails fused together by rust. He had small sharp gooseberry eyes under straight brows, an aggressive nose, and fine hair plastered to his forehead in the classical style. He had on a fresh collar and there was something of the uniform in the way he wore his clawhammer coat and vest with no chain or decoration of any kind.

"Have a seat, Deputy. How is my old friend Harlan Blackthorne?"

"He's well, General. Your honor. He sends his regards." The horsehair chair felt strange after the hard seats in the day coach. No Pullmans for a deputy United States marshal from Montana Territory.

The office was done up in that Spanish frontier style I'd gotten my first taste of the moment I crossed into New Mexico Territory and had my fill of long before I reached Santa Fe: brick-reinforced adobe, squaw rugs on a pine floor, and an oak desk as big as a porch with leather stretched drum tight across the top and secured with brass tacks the size of ten-dollar gold pieces. A walnut bookcase with glass doors contained mustard-bound law books, Bowdler's Gibbon, and at least ten copies of *Ben Hur*.

At the window overlooking the plaza stood a beanpole in a ready-made suit, all elbows and Adam's apple, a big-eared, knob-knuckled Missouri farmer got up for Sunday with pomade in his hair and moustache. He was as red as a skinned rabbit and looked hard on fifty, which in that country meant he was closer to thirty. He regarded me with pale unfriendly eyes and made no move my way when Wallace introduced us.

"Page Murdock, this is Pat Garrett. Garrett's sheriff in Lincoln County."

"Hard place." I didn't recognize his name, although it was clear from the governor's tone I was supposed to.

Garrett said nothing. Wallace lowered himself into his leather swivel. "Mr. Garrett's here for my advice. Not as a politician or as a military man, but as an author. He's considering a book about his experiences and he has it in his mind I know something about the subject because of my little tale of the Christ." He was being modest. *Ben Hur* had been on sale barely a year and already shared a shelf with the Bible in most of the homes I'd visited.

I raised my brows politely. "Experiences?"

"Mr. Garrett shot and killed Billy the Kid last month down in Fort Sumner."

I shook my head, feeling ignorant. Wallace stared, then sat back slightly and twitched his shoulders. "You wouldn't have heard of him up in your country, I suppose. The little bucktoothed killer put us through six kinds of perdition after that circus in Lincoln County." He looked at Garrett. "Mr. Murdock rides for Judge Blackthorne up north. His employer and I served together in Mexico. He was a fierce campaigner then and if what I hear from Helena is true, he hasn't changed a great deal."

Garrett was back looking out the window. I said, "He speaks well of your military record too, your honor. General." What the Judge, who had also known the New Mexico governor when he was prosecuting the conspirators in the assassination of President Lincoln, had actually said was that as a lawyer Wallace proved a consummate soldier. He'd added that he couldn't write, either.

Wallace blushed exactly like a girl and fingered his whiskers. "I asked my publishers to send him a copy of the book. Did he read it?"

"Yes, sir. He said it was a splendid example of the current condition of American letters."

"Yes. Well." He cleared his throat. "Was there anything else, Mr. Garrett?"

The sheriff from Lincoln County said he guessed there wasn't and excused himself. His petal-soft Alabama drawl didn't go with the rest of him. He left without having spoken to me once and I never heard anything more from him until his book came out a year or so later. I read it and made up my mind there and then never to write one. One more promise I haven't managed to keep.

Wallace tugged a yellow telegraph flimsy out of a sheaf pinned to his desk by a bronze bust of Alexander and straddled his nose with a pair of egg-shaped spectacles to read it. "Harlan's wire says to expect you and to show you the same courtesy I would him. It says nothing else. I assume you're in Santa Fe on business."

"Yes and no, General. Your honor."

" 'Your honor' is sufficient. I sent down the uniform after Appomattox. Which is it, yes or no?" He socked the spectacles into an oystershell case and snapped it shut.

"Well, it's business but not law business. I'm no longer in government service."

"How old are you?"

"Forty next month." I had to fish for it. I wasn't expecting the question.

"Only fancy men and laggards retire before age sixty. You don't dress well enough for the former and for a man who just spent forty-six hours on the rails you still move too quickly to pass for indolent. Were you dismissed?"

"Forty-eight," I corrected. "We hit a cow. I handed in my badge and papers."

"Differences, after all this time? Judge Blackthorne's wire says you've been with him six years. I'll warrant he's a difficult man, but surely by now—"

"Your honor, I'm too tired for tact. It isn't my strong suit when I'm fresh. I stand a whole lot less chance of tangling myself in my tongue if I speak directly."

"Please do."

I sat forward, resting my forearms on the desktop.

I saw then what he meant about not dressing gay enough to be kept by a woman with cash. The one good suit of clothes I wore for court and genteel travel needed brushing and my shirtcuffs were as raveled as old crepe. "Bear Anderson was a difficult man. You wouldn't have caught wind of him down here any more than I heard of your Billy the Kid. The Flathead Indians, what he left of them, were ready to stop hunting him and make him into a god when I pulled him down out of the Bitterroot Mountains four years ago and stood him on a scaffold. A one-eyed buffalo bull with a belly full of crazy weed and an arrowhead stuck under its tail is difficult. Judge Blackthorne is the cruellest, pigheadedest, most vindictive and contrary mother's son that ever trod cobble. That wasn't bad enough but some damn fool in Washington City saw fit to put a gavel in his hand and place him in sole charge of a territory bigger than most countries. It didn't improve his temperament."

He might have smiled behind the beard. I couldn't tell for sure but there was humor in the sharp eyes, or what passed for it in that old-soldier circle. "And so you feel you've had your life's portion of Harlan A. Blackthorne and all his works."

"It isn't just that. What with the war and trail herding and upholding the duly constituted law between Canada and old Mexico I've spent the best part of the last twenty years either too hot or too cold or too shot at, and most of it horseback. I'd like to try a town job for a while. I'm a fair hand with cards and I've been offered the chance to buy a half interest in a saloon down in Socorro County."

"Congratulations, Deputy. That's good cattle country and they're prospecting for silver in the vicinity. You should do a fair trade. Unfortunately, I don't gamble and I've never trafficked in spirits. Just what is it you're expecting of me?"

"I'm not expecting anything, Governor. The Judge and I parted on friendly terms and he offered to put in a good word with you in honor of our long association. I'm told there's been trouble in Socorro County and the sheriff there has blocked the establishment of any new saloons until it sorts itself out. My partner, Junior Harper, doesn't feel that order will affect our transaction as the Apache Princess has been operating for six months, but the Judge thought I might benefit from a letter of reference signed by the governor of New Mexico Territory, just in case."

"Attesting that you are a man of family and good character."

"The character part, anyway," I said. "I never did find tracks in that family country."

He sat back again, not far, gripping the arms of his swivel. All those drills had pounded into him the posture of a Springfield rifle. "Word travels faster down here than you suppose, Deputy. Allow me to show you a popular item available at the mercantile down the street. I would that my book sold as well." He took something out of the top drawer of the desk and placed it on top, square in the middle.

It was a pamphlet, bound in dirty yellow paper the size of a newspaper folded in quarters but not as thick. The cover bore a steelpoint engraving of a fierce fork-bearded jasper straddling a lathered horse. He had the reins clamped between his teeth and a hogleg belching fire in each hand. Ran the legend:

SATAN'S SIXGUN:
Being a True and Authentic Account
of the Adventures of Page Murdock,
the Lawless Lawman of Helena.
By Jack Rimfire

I grinned at the illustration. "I can't wear whiskers," I said. "I tried but they come in all colors."

"Are you acquainted with this fellow Rimfire?"

"Aaron Hookstratton's his right name. I ran him
out of Helena last year after I shot Jordan Mercy. He
was running a medicine show and seemed determined to foment a rebellion over Mercy. It sounds
just like that counterfeit colonel to take his revenge in
this way."

Wallace sat silent for a long time. Then he jerked
his head in a manner I took to be positive. "A good
answer. Had you denied knowing him I might have
assigned weight to his tale. There was either truth or
bad blood behind it."

"Does that mean you'll provide the letter of reference?"

"Nothing would give me greater pleasure than to
grant Judge Blackthorne's request. It's a rare enough
thing for him to make one." He fished a gunmetal
watch out of his vest. "Where are you stopping in
town? I'll have the letter delivered tomorrow."

"Don't trouble yourself, your honor." I slid the
cowhide wallet out of my coat, removed the letter the
Judge had dictated, and spread it out on top of the
nickel novel on the desk. It was damp from the long
ride plastered to my ribs.

He put on his spectacles. "Indeed. Most glowing. I

see he employs a type-writer. I had no idea the nineteenth century was so firmly entrenched that far north."

"His niece took a course in Chicago."

"Comely, no doubt. I knew his wife when he was courting her."

"She's his sister's child."

"Oh." He unstuck his pen from the blotter, dipped it, and signed his name to the bottom of the letter. "I won't guarantee its efficacy in Socorro County," he said, sprinkling sand on the ink from a little glass container bearing the United States seal. "Frank Baronet is the sheriff. He and his twin brother Ross rode for the Dolan-Murphy syndicate during the late unpleasantness in Lincoln County. Ross was wounded in a raid on a ranch house that left a small cattleman and his wife slain and is believed to be either recovering and in hiding or dead somewhere below the border. No witnesses came forward to connect Frank to the raid but he rode off anyway and got himself elected down there; Jimmy Dolan has friends all over the territory and they throw a wide loop. My predecessor was a Dolan man. You can draw from that the extent of my influence in that country."

I thanked him for the letter and put it away. "I shouldn't have too many dealings with him after this one. He's in Socorro City and the Apache Princess is in San Sábado."

Rising from his seat, he hesitated. "That is a harsh place to spend your retirement from law enforcement. The town has a rough history. It's sheltered bandits and revolutionaries since the time of Cortez. Three times in the past, vendettas have wiped out its male population. The Mexicans call it *La Ciudad de Las Viudas.*"

I stood. "I didn't get much opportunity to practice my Spanish up in Montana."

"It means The City of Widows." He extended a grave hand. "Go with God, Deputy."

**≈ 2 ≈**

Sheriff's Office
Socorro County
City of Socorro, N.M.T.
Aug. 15, 1881
Mr. _____:
Your Presence is requested at the Execution of
    HERNANDO PADILLA
For the Murder of Ernestine "Mexican Red"
Grosvenor. To take place in the Yard of the
Socorro County Jail on
            Monday, August 22, 1881.
                (signed)
        FRANCIS S. K. BARONET, Sheriff

About a dozen of the invitations, printed on
coarse gray stock with a black border, stood in a pile
on the yellow oak counter separating the customer's
side of the office from the side where the serious busi-

ness was conducted. It was a big swept room smelling of oiled wood and sun, uncluttered, with lath and plaster over the adobe and two big brick-framed windows in front. The door to a hallway leading to the cells in back stood open. There were two desks with chairs and a big worktable supporting a parchment-colored map of the county, its corners held down by odd office items and an empty tequila bottle. Wanted readers and telegraph flimsies layered a corkboard like shingles and a buffalo gun with an octagonal barrel shared a wall rack with matched Winchesters, a Henry, and a Stevens ten-gauge cut back to within an inch of its usefulness. It looked like every other place on the frontier where the local law was upheld. I think I must have missed the issue of *Harper's Weekly* that set the standard.

"Go ahead."

It occurred to me as I turned that I was getting out of marshaling just in time. I hadn't heard the owner of the voice coming in behind me. He was at least half Indian, or all Mexican, which that close to Chihuahua amounted to the same thing. Short, thick, and brown, he had eyes as black and shiny as beetles in slits without lashes and a wide mouth with triangles of moustache at the corners. He wore a Stetson the way it had come from the factory, with neither dent nor dimple in the crown and as flat in the brim as a tortilla, a clean white shirt buttoned to the throat, and striped trousers reinforced with leather and stuffed into the tops of stovepipe boots. His age was indeterminate. A Smith & Weston .44, the Russian, with the slim black rubber grip and a bow spur on the trigger guard, rode high on his hip in a left-handed holster and he was carrying a Remington Creedmoor rifle with a folding sight. The brass star on his shirt bore no engraving.

"Go ahead," he repeated, "take one. Be sure and fill in your name before you present it."

I said, "I don't expect to be in town on the twenty-second. Do you always give out invitations to whoever blows in?"

"Not as a matter of general practice. The sheriff likes a good crowd for a hanging—he says that's what separates a lynching from a legal execution—but Nando was the town barber and a good one and nobody much wants to see him dangle. Jury might not have convicted him except the town needs whores more than it needs barbers. Mexican Red had a following." He leaned his rifle in the corner by the front door. "You'd be the fellow from the train. Oz Alanson at the freight office seen three people get off. You don't look like a pipe drummer from Detroit and you sure ain't Ernst Schwimmer's wife Gretchen."

"Page Murdock." I grasped a hard sandy palm with more strength in it than he was bothering to employ. "If you're Frank Baronet, I have a letter for you."

He showed me two gold teeth. "Hell, you ain't that much bigger than me. What kind of wages is that Satan paying these days?"

"I hoped that hadn't got down this far." At that moment I wanted that half-dime novelist standing in front of me more than a woman.

"Oh, we get all the latest since the A.T. and S.F. came through. The name's Jubilo, I'm the full-time deputy. This time of day you'll find Mr. Baronet at the Orient. He owns the game there."

"Just Jubilo?"

His face now looked as if any smile that tried to light there would curl up and blow away. "I don't use the other. It was just my mother's."

I thanked him for the information and went out to find the Orient.

Walking felt good after another eighteen hours in the cars. I'd dropped off my necessaries at a hotel named for the town and county, visited a bathhouse that brushed suits while you washed, and with a shave and a change of shirts I felt closer to civilized man than I had at any time since Montana. My interview with Governor Wallace in Santa Fe had been just brief enough to allow me to catch the next train south, which was how my luck had been running lately.

Socorro City showed all the signs of a town on the grow. Buckboards and buggies outnumbered saddle horses on the street. Frame buildings were clattering up among the adobe and lumber was stacked everywhere, some of it under armed guard because by the time it was cut and milled in the mountains to the west and transported by wagon to the building sites it was worth nearly as much as a shipment of silver. Four men in shirtsleeves and paint-drizzled overalls were at work in front of a sign shop, where a dozen fresh placards were already curing against the side of the building. Most of them seemed to advertise real estate brokers. There were a stove works, a billiard hall, and four saloons on a main street as wide as a pasture. Prospectors came there for supplies and trail herders stopped there to cut the dust on their way across the border to borrow cattle from the old Spanish grandees.

The pride of the Orient, and likely the inspiration for its name, seemed to be a paneled bar as long as an express car, lacquered black with cherry blossoms painted on the front. Antelope heads decorated the back wall and a six-foot painting of a belly dancer in a frame crusted over with gilt cupids dominated one end of a room built along the lines of a shotgun to accommodate a narrow lot. At that afternoon hour all the tables were occupied. When I asked for Frank Baronet a bartender with a strawberry mark on his forehead and a bulldog pistol standing in a water tumbler at his right elbow pointed out the faro table.

"You playing?" he asked.

"Not today."

"You'd best wait then till he finishes off that fellow. When it comes to kibitzers Frank is no Christian. There's an empty chair at that corner table if you're drinking. Billy the Kid sat there when he shot Feeny MacAdo last December. Straight through the heart at fifty-four feet."

"This Kid must have been hell on a stick. It can't be twenty feet from there to the door."

"Nineteen and a half. Feeny was eating his breakfast in the Chicago House across the street when Fate struck him down."

I left the corner table to the Kid's ghost and went over to watch the game.

A sallow-faced man in a bowler and fresh collar that made his skin look even more unhealthy was bucking the tiger. He had a large stack of chips and eyes that never left the board except to follow the dealer's movements when he slid a counter in the cue box. The dealer was as lean as a lodgepole and sat as stiffly, with an embroidered pillow doubled behind his back for support. He was sheathed in a black vest and green-striped shirtsleeves with garters to match the stripes and parted his black hair in the center. He had modest handlebars, a predatory nose, and an odd habit of batting his eyelids rapidly, like a sporting lady. It seemed a clumsy signaling device, but as there was no one standing behind the player I assumed it was some kind of tic. They say Jesse James suffered from a similar affliction.

A counter moved. The player studied the board, sucked on his cigar. He put it down and slid a stack of reds onto the five of spades. The dealer drew two cards out of the box and laid them face up on the table. The first was the deuce of hearts. The second was the five of spades.

The dealer exhaled softly. "Sid, you are part Irish today. I never saw such a run."

"How many turns left?" Sid asked.

"Nine."

"Wrong again, Frank. It's ten."

"Well, why the hell did you ask if you knew the answer?"

"I got a side bet with Lyle Ring on just how big a liar you are." He moved his chips to another card. "Draw again."

"Sheriff Baronet?" I said.

The dealer winced and reached back to adjust his pillow. Three points of a nickel-plated star poked out of a pocket in his vest. "Later, mister. I have just ten more chances to bust this gentleman out. After that you just might be bringing your business to Sheriff Sidney L. Boone."

I recognized the name. "The real estate broker. I think your sign's done."

The player picked up his cigar and drew on it. His attention remained on the board.

"I'm Page Murdock," I told Baronet. "I guess you know me better around here as Satan's Sixgun."

"Give me a minute, Sid." The player shrugged and sat back smoking and glowering at the board. Baronet blinked, regarding me. "You're a lot south of your pasture, Marshal. We've had our sorrows with that cow crowd, getting drunk and shooting up innocent greasers they take for Don Segundo's vaqueros, but we are on top of it. It never was a federal matter."

"That's all behind me," I said. "I'm fixed to go into private enterprise in San Sábado. Junior Harper has sold me half of the Apache Princess. I'm here to see if that's all right with Socorro County."

"You no longer keep the peace?"

"Only my own."

He counted his chips. His other hand dangled off the back of his chair near the pillow. "I'm concerned about this yellowback business. It might draw fire. Some pissant *pistolero* reads his nickel's worth and decides to find out for himself if you sizzle on the griddle. He shoots you or you shoot him. Either way somebody has to dig a hole. The newspapers forget all about Tombstone and here I am sitting on six hundred thousand square miles of sand and scorpion shit and no prospects. It's happened in milder places than this."

"Maybe they'll decide to publish this instead." I
handed him Governor Wallace's letter.

He read it quickly and handed it back. "That carpetbagger. Things were just becoming settled in Lincoln County when he brought in the federals and
stirred them back up. It killed my brother, Ross."

"I heard he was wounded in some kind of raid."

"He ran wild, I don't deny it. Ross hadn't my temperament or he would not have lashed out. He died
last month of the blood fever in a cave in Chihuahua."

"I saw him three weeks ago in Juarez," Sid Boone
said. "He looked fit to me."

"You're mistaken." Baronet batted his eyes at me.
"I went through there on my way to bury Ross. We
were twins. People confused us often."

"Ross is two inches shorter and twenty pounds
heavier. I guess I can tell you apart."

"Someone else, then."

I put away the letter. "What about the partnership?"

"The Princess has a quiet reputation," Baronet
said. "Anyway the ordinance against any new saloons expired last week. I look forward to trying my
luck at your table."

I thanked him, hesitated. "How large is the caliber
in that pillow?"

He had good teeth behind the moustaches, blue-
white against the New Mexico tan. From behind the
embroidered pillow he drew a Remington Rolling
Block pistol with a fifty-caliber bore. I could have

reached inside with my fingers and plucked out the ball.

"I didn't know buffalo came this far down," I said.

"Single-shot." He turned it sideways, admiring its lazy-J lines. "I've found that in indoor shooting, one slug this size is sufficient. What's that you carry?"

I pulled aside my coattail to show the chicken-bone butt of the five-shot in the dropover holster. "Deane-Adams. English gun. It fires Colt's forty-five, but only if I load the cartridges myself."

"Frank." Sid Boone put out his cigar.

The sheriff laid down the Remington and dealt two cards. I thanked him again and left.

The Socorro Hotel was one of the older adobe structures on a side street. My room was cool in the daytime desert heat but included a scooped-out fireplace for the chilly evenings. A Navajo saddle blanket did for a rug on the planks. There was a crucifix on the wall above the iron bedstead and a cornshuck mattress that felt like spun clouds when I stretched out on it in my clothes, and to hell with the rustling and scratching when I turned over. A Mexican as old as cornmeal and frijoles, shriveled down no bigger than my thumb in peasant cotton and rope sandals that slapped his feet like shutters, came in at sundown with an armload of sticks and started a fire. When he left I got one boot off and dropped into the warmest blackest hole I had been in since childhood.

I woke up just after dawn, feeling sore all over and more rested than I had at any time since quitting Helena. I thought about treating myself to a barber shave, then remembered that Hernando Padilla was in jail thinking about his own neck, and shaved myself. I put on corduroys, a fresh shirt, and a mackinaw against the morning cold and reported for breakfast to the Chicago House, where Feeny MacAdo had had the black fortune to sit in the line of Billy the Kid's magic fire.

I had a short wait. The room, plastered and wainscoted, with framed lithographs of Greek ruins leaning out from the walls, was just big enough for six tables and was clearly the most popular place to eat in town. At length I was seated by the owner, a bald, loose-jowled German in his fifties whose waistline was his best advertising. He brought out my steak and eggs in good order and filled my cup from an old campaigner of a two-gallon pot.

"Big doings at the Orient last night, you bet," he said. "You heard shooting?"

"Last night I'd have slept through Shiloh." The coffee was thick and black and strong enough to float a fifty-cent piece. It scorched a furrow all the way down to my stomach. "Who got shot?"

"Sid Boone, the real property man. They are saying he had a bad run at the sheriff's table and went on the prod. He took out his pistol. Mr. Baronet put a round in him while he was still cocking. He is dead as Judas."

He spotted an empty cup and boated off before I could ask questions.

My steak had had all the fight pounded out of it. Cutting it up, I reflected on how rapidly a man's luck could change in a game of chance.

## 3

THE SUN WAS barely above the Oscuros when I stepped out of the Chicago House and already the heat was crawling off the dirt street. It lay across my shoulders like an oak beam when I took off the mackinaw.

The larger of the town's two liveries was an unpainted barn with a roof that extended four feet past the front, throwing a triangle of shade on a man sitting on a bench in overalls with one strap gone, brogans with black steel toes poking through the leather, and a slouch hat with no more shape than a bar rag. He was shirtless and the hair on his chest was pale against the boiled skin.

"I need a saddle horse for a couple of hours," I said. "What's the best you've got?"

He had to tip his head all the way back to see up from under his flop brim. He was a towheaded twenty, a surprise. He had slat shoulders and the general dilapidated posture of a man in his seventies.

CITY OF WIDOWS                    31

"Depends on what you want it for. I got a buckskin wouldn't throw a child or a fly but you'd have to
carry it back from the lip of town on your hip."

"It has to carry me out to the Whiteside ranch and
back. No flies or children."

His head dropped. "Patch get you."

"I heard the Apaches were raiding Arizona this
year."

"Patch don't know when he's across the line." He
spat. The spittle evaporated in the air.

"I'm obliged for your time," I said, turning.
"There's another stable."

"Don't get your bowels in an uproar, mister. She's
too hot to argue." He stood, stretched, and went inside. The sun moved, and then he came back out
leading a gaunt bay by its bridle. Its hip sockets
showed and its right eye was milky.

"That's as good as it gets?"

"Good as *you* get anyway. You don't have to stand
in front of my uncle and tell him Patch et his sorrel for
noon dinner." He tipped his head. "What's that for?"

I had drawn the Deane-Adams. I plugged a cartridge into the empty chamber and spun the cylinder
with a diamondback buzz. "I want to be sure I have
enough shells to hit a swift-moving target like you
once I finish putting this sack of umbrellas out of its
misery."

"Hold on, mister. There's law in this county."

"Curious thing about the law. It almost always
gets off the second shot." I holstered the revolver.
"Ten minutes from now I'm going to step out the
front door of the Socorro Hotel and throw a leg over
an animal with some kind of pulse. If I should fall off

the porch for lack of anything to break my drop, the law in this county is going to hold an inquest over your remains. That's if it can find a difference."

"Two dollars for the day," he said after a minute. "Saddle's fifty cents extra."

"I'll use my own." I handed him two cartwheels and left.

A sorrel with some years left on it was hitched at the rail when I came out carrying my gear. The boy was there and so was Frank Baronet. The sheriff had on a Prince Albert and a pinch hat squared over his brows. His thumbs were hooked inside the armholes of his vest and the gutta-percha handle of the large-bore Remington poked out of the notch above his belt buckle. He looked like an election poster.

He blinked up at the sky. "There's worse days for a ride."

"Not in Montana." I set down the saddle and Winchester and smoothed my faded blanket over the horse's back. "Is it always like this?"

"Nine months out of the year. Then it heats up."

I slung the saddle into place, jerked the cinch before the animal could puff itself up. It whickered and tried to crawl out of its skin. "I heard you had a row."

"Yes sir, I did. I'm going to miss old Sid. It's sad what the love of money will do to a Christian."

"The cards must have gone sour for him all at once. He was a piece ahead when I left."

"They will do that. I won back the table stakes plus an interest in his real business when he got frisky with that belly gun he carried. His widow can keep the store. I only let him wager it because he was determined to quit even. If I knew how determined I'd have shut down the game."

"I guess you had a crowd by then. When a man loses that much that fast it generally draws an audience."

"No, it was late. It was just Sid and me and Mike Henry behind the bar. Mike was asleep on his hand at the time. He fell off it and chipped a tooth when I fired."

"You're proficient with that buffalo pistol."

"I was elected to keep the peace. I don't play at it." He blinked. "I'll have that hip gun."

When a man says that, right out of the blue with both hands occupied, you look around. Jubilo, the deputy sheriff with no last name, was standing at the end of the hotel porch with his Creedmoor rifle resting on top of the railing. The bottom half of his face was a desert beneath the shadow of his flat brim. At that range he didn't need the folding sight.

I looked back at Baronet. "I'm headed into Apache country."

"You should have thought of that before you threatened the life of young Ole here. I'll have the whole rig. Just hang it over the hitch."

I unbuckled the cartridge belt and draped it next to the sorrel's tie. The sheriff stepped forward and lifted it off. "Hang on to that." He thrust it at the boy, who seized it eagerly, his head tilted back to watch me. His face was all anticipation.

"You don't wear the tin, you don't abuse a free man." Baronet jerked the Remington out of his belt and backhanded it in the same motion. A drop of red paint on the front sight caught my eye just before the sun exploded. I missed the fall. I was lying on the porch boards looking at the remains of my steak and eggs.

"Aw." Ole was disgusted. "He got something on my pants."

I rolled over quickly. The sole of a boot fastened on my throat.

"Come around here waving a letter from the governor," Baronet said. "I kill a man, I don't eat for three days. You can thank Sid Boone for your life, him and the fact I don't take to starvation. Otherwise you'd be bucking the devil's tiger right along with him."

"Aw, kill him."

"Shut up, Ole."

I was having trouble squeezing wind down my pipe. The sheriff leaned in, shutting off the rest of the supply. I clutched at his boot, but the blow to my head had done something to my connections. I had no feeling in my fingers.

"There's one law in Socorro." His upper body blocked the light. "It isn't a yellowback former federal named Murdock and it sure isn't that carpetbagging Wallace in Santa Fe. Let me hear you say its name."

I couldn't talk. He leaned harder. My vision broke up into black-and-white checks.

"Say its name."

The white checks shrank to pinholes. I could feel the blood swelling the veins in my eyeballs.

He leaned back then, relieving some of the pressure. I sucked in air and coughed.

"Frank Baronet."

He removed his foot, straightened. His face was an

oval blur inside the circle of his hatbrim with sharp blue sky behind it.

" 'Satan's Sixgun,' " he said. "My ass."

I lay there for a space of time. I knew Baronet had left and probably Ole and the deputy, but I was aware that I was still an object of curiosity for a portion of the local tax base. My hands were starting to tingle when I pushed myself into a sitting position. My cartridge belt slid off my chest and the Deane-Adams clunked against the boards. I hadn't even felt its weight when it was dumped on me.

I picked it up along with myself, found my hat, Winchester and canteen, and went back inside to use the basin in my room. The barrel of the sheriff's pistol hadn't broken the skin but the entire right side of my head felt like rotten wood. I inspected the loads in the five-shot, gripped the handle hard until I could feel it as far as my elbow. I brushed the sawdust off my corduroys and went out.

The countryside was ablaze with that dry heat that opens your pores and sucks out the moisture like lemon carbonate through a straw. For all that it was a green land, dotted over with juniper and scrub oak connecting in the distance to create the illusion of a grass ocean. The mountains too were flecked with green, cloud-capped, the air so clear around them I might have been looking at them through a glass. The sky came down to the ground.

The ranch road led past a long low adobe house with a red tile roof and a corral next to it containing half a dozen horses. Behind the house I found a Mexican cook and his Negro helper scalding a hog in a cauldron the size of a bathtub. The cook said I'd find *Señor* Whiteside stringing fence in the northwest corner. I didn't waste time leaving the pair to their work. I don't mind the smell of singed bristles, but a dead hog looks too much like a naked man to my taste. On my way back to the road I paused to look over the horses in the corral.

John Whiteside is in most of the history books now as the man who opened up New Mexico to the cattle trade. Severely wounded at the head of his own regiment at Cold Harbor and mustered out, he got a head start on the other barons who went west after the war, rounding up the red-eyed, ladder-ribbed descendants of Cortez's longhorns wandering wild in Mexico and booting them up into the territories, inventing a new business in the process. Comanches raped and killed his Mexican wife of six months and ran off his first herd, and when he got through fighting them the Apaches came and burned his headquarters and strung his partner head down over a mesquite fire until his brains boiled. Whiteside was still fighting them at the time I caught up with him in the summer of 1881, but his fame had not yet spread north of Taos and I didn't know him from General Grant. He was just a short twist of rawhide seated on a wagon loaded with spools of barbed wire in a faded blue flannel shirt, canvas breeches, and a wide Mexican sombrero, holding the team while a trio of men in overalls and leather gauntlets spun the jacked-up left rear wheel to seat the wire around a fencepost. He had brown whiskers going gray around his mouth and restless blue eyes in a thicket of wrinkles. His left arm was gone above the elbow, the empty sleeve pinned back.

"I require all the horses I have." He'd glanced at me when I rode up, then returned to his seemingly aimless study of the horizon. If an irregularity appeared there he'd spot it.

"I'm no hand at bargaining," I said. "The truth is I stink at it. I'll pay two hundred for that claybank in the corral."

"Murdock, is it? Mr. Murdock, I'm in the fence business. I used to trade in cattle but right now I spend most of my time restringing wire. I've strung this section six times. Billy the Kid showed the world how easy it is last October when he cut it the first time and spirited out five hundred head. Between the goddamn thieves and those Apache bastards and that greaser son of a bitch Don Segundo del Guerrero down in Chihuahua and every lost tramp who cannot be bothered to ride half a mile to the nearest gate I have strung more wire in this one corner than Western Union. You will pardon me if I don't feel the necessity to add a livery operation to this here booming fence trade I have going."

"The sheriff gave me your name."

"Sheriff." He snarled the word. "Dolan men counted the ballots. They were only just through counting when the first silver shipment to the bank in Socorro City went missing. It was Frank's brother Ross done it and he has been behind all the others since. I supply beef to all the bigger mining companies in the territory and what injures them injures me. When I suggested taking this to Lew Wallace, Frank started arresting my best hands for shooting up Mexicans."

"He said something about it. He didn't say your men were involved."

"My hands were swapping lead with Don Segundo's vaqueros over the ownership of cows when the Baronet brothers were still abusing themselves to cigarette cards. Anyway I took his message. It isn't my silver, and I need men to run a ranch."

"You must have choked on it."

"It wasn't my first choice. However, times are different. Sooner or later some ass would decide to call in the army just like they done in Lincoln County. That is bad for business."

"The fence business." I grinned.

He turned his blues on me. They were as austere as the sky. "I see someone has used you."

I let the grin slide. "Baronet. I was foolish enough to give him a reason, but his real purpose was to warn me. I was there last night when a man named Boone caught him in a lie about his brother being dead in Mexico. He killed Boone later. He said it was an argument over cards, but he was the only witness."

"I don't mourn Sidney L. Boone. Those land men are slicing up the country like a steer. Are you fixing to call Frank out?"

"Fights are easy enough come by without provoking them. Anyway I haven't time. I'm just passing through on my way to San Sábado."

"What's in the Widow City?"

"A place called the Apache Princess, and my signature on the operating agreement. Cattlemen welcome. Fence men too," I added. "What about that claybank?"

His attention hesitated on something, then moved on. An antelope or a low cloud.

"Three hundred," he said. "This wire costs money when you order it by the carload."

We shook on it.

## 4

"Well, Murdock, I guess you have had your fill of the county seat."

I exhaled slowly, letting some of the tension out with the bad air. After checking out of the hotel and packing my worldly possessions aboard my new mount I had hoped to clear the place without running into the sheriff. I'd begun to think I might succeed when I pulled over to let a buggy pass coming in from the east road and Frank Baronet drew rein to blink up at me from under the roof. He had on a linen duster over his town clothes and a Henry rifle that might have been the one I'd seen in the county office leaning against his thigh. The embroidered pillow was wedged between his lower back and the leather seat. I had dismissed that as a ploy to conceal his pistol, but since the handle of the Remington was visible in the notch of his vest I decided the pillow served another purpose.

"I've been in town less than a day and already there's been a killing and a pistol-whipping," I said. "I left marshaling to get away from that."

"If that was your intention you should have gone back East, where I hear a man can wet his beak of a Saturday evening without a weapon on his person." His eyes went to the claybank's brand. "I see you took my advice and went to Whiteside. What that man knows about horses and cattle comes close to making up for what he don't know about people."

It was a conversation I didn't feel like getting into. "When I saw that rig I thought you were a doctor." It was a handsome construction of pebbled black oilskin and good leather on yellow wheels, hitched to a patient-looking gray. Brass fittings caught the light.

"A walleyed mustang threw me into a ravine in '78. I haven't been able to ride more than eight or ten miles at a stretch since the brace came off. Misery of the back is a hellish thing, worse than being shot. It has taken all the fun out of collecting taxes." He adjusted the pillow and leaned back. Pain brushed across his features like a cloud. "Don't forget to register with the marshal's office when you get to San Sábado. It is required of new saloon owners."

"Your order?"

He spread his moustaches. "When it's one of mine I enforce it with enthusiasm, as I think you know." He gathered the reins. "*Buena suerte,* Murdock. I will be in one day soon and try my luck at your table." He rattled off.

My destination was a day's ride from Socorro City in gentle weather, slightly longer in the dead-blow hammer heat of August. The way led south along the foothills of the Oscuros and San Andres, broken peaks bleached white above the timberline like the molars of fighting dogs, through a region covered with cactus nettles and white alkali, charmingly named *La Jornada del Muerto*. I kept a weather eye, but of course I didn't see Apaches. There never were enough of them in any one place to make a show of strength on a ridge like in the five-cent dreadfuls. Their strategy was to run among the rocks like those little hot-blooded lizards you saw in the tail of your eye and take you from behind. At dusk I made camp in the lee of an old rockfall with the claybank tethered to my wrist and my Winchester across my lap. In the morning I found the charred foundation of a house nearby and the rocky oblongs of four graves, their markers long since gone if there had been any to begin with. It was raw country, stolen many times from determined hands at great cost. The white man was only the latest in a long line of misguided thieves.

You don't haggle too hard over the price of a good horse in country where your life depends on what you're riding, and the claybank was proving to be a wise investment. It was a gelding, fifteen hands high with a big rump and an arrogant manner, which meant a keen sense of self-preservation. This last was a credit, as a suicidal horse is less than useful when scalp fever is abroad. Of course the beast hated me. All my mounts do out of instinct. They know I'll shoot them for a breastwork the minute we fall short of room to run.

Not missing San Sábado entirely required knowledge of the ways of open country. Coming over a rise I saw what looked at first like Indian mounds or a prairie dog town, but was in fact a collection of adobe buildings swept up around the base of a sixteenth-century mission, with a few frame structures strag-gled east like a thread unraveling, and everything baked the same dun color on a flat that hadn't known shade since the last glacier. Something inside me sank at the sight. I felt like the consumptive who had come at last to the place where he would die, and it wasn't Atlantic City, New Jersey.

Closer up, things were more encouraging. The bell in the mission tower began to swing, the thud of its clapper humming along the ground and shaking loose activity behind windows and inside the covered walkways. That would be the end of the noon siesta. There was, in addition to another saloon besides the Apache Princess, a livery, an emporium, and a combi-nation bathhouse and barbershop, the last in a build-ing that had started out adobe, then split in the middle like some kind of hybrid grass and wound up clapboard with a shake roof. Best of all, a harness shop advertised itself in two windows on the second floor of the livery. That meant cowboys. The bare fact that I would welcome that obstreperous lot was evi-dence enough I had stopped thinking like a lawman and started thinking like an entrepreneur.

Other windows, particularly those in the old mud huts, were less cheering. Muslin curtains stirred but did not open. Behind two of them I glimpsed the black weeds of the widows who gave the town its popular name.

I stepped down in front of the livery, removed my necessaries from behind the cantle, and told the Yaquí who came out from inside to rub down the claybank and give it water and feed. The Indian, short and thick in peasant dress with his hair cut short and no shine in his black eyes, took the reins and said nothing. That breed got most of its talking and all of its laughing done by age ten.

THE APACHE PRINCESS was painted in circus letters two feet high across the windowless false front of the last wooden building in the row. They would have flared out in bright barn red when they were new, but in just six months the New Mexico sun had dulled them the color of dried blood. I pushed aside a half-door on a leather hinge and stood inside the dim interior, blinking like Frank Baronet. The sudden shade chilled the back of my neck.

"Page! Goddamn!" A chair scraped back and my hand was seized by a narrow wiry one crackling with nervous energy. "The red bastards didn't scalp you after all. There's a bet won."

"It's good to see you, Junior."

I did see him now, all five and a half skinny feet of him, splendid in lilac-colored shirtsleeves with red plush garters, paisley vest, and a green silk cravat stuck with a ruby pin. His collar was too big by half and his fingers stuck out of the cuffs like a child's. He looked as out of place in the rig as he had in range clothes when we both worked his father's spread in Montana. Junior Harper had fair hair darkened with pomade and slicked flat to his skull, large luminous eyes, and a long rectangular jaw like a sewing machine treadle that slid to the side rakishly when he showed his big horse teeth. At first glance, and maybe at all the others, he looked like a hereditary failure beside Ford Harper's bull shoulders and red beard shot through with iron gray, and in fact two physicians, including a specialist whom Ford had brought in from Saint Louis for a second opinion, had predicted Junior wouldn't live to see twenty; but he had made them both liars by fifteen years and counting and there wasn't a hand who had worked with him who didn't have some story attesting to his strength and endurance. He was a pale reed with a taproot that went clear through to China.

"You're some older," he said, stepping back to take me in from hat to heels, "but you are still one mean-looking son of a bitch. I'm guessing Geronimo took one look at you and hared right back to Arizona."

"You look like Christmas Day. Is that what they're wearing on the border this year?"

He grinned his sloppy sideways grin and stuck a hand inside his vest like an oil painting. "Men of property don't dress like spring roundup. I hope you aren't fixing to deal cards in that kit."

"I had a suit fitted before I left Helena. It's probably following me right now. Is your mother still living?" I remembered a frail brown sparrow, small-boned like her son and withered beyond her years in Ford's shadow.

"She's well and in Chicago. She moved in with my aunt after the old man died. You heard he was dead."

"Apoplexy, I heard." My bet had been on either the Shoshones or a fall from a mad horse. He'd continued to insist on breaking his share of the string well past his sixtieth birthday.

"I sold the ranch to pay his debts. Ma got most of

the rest and I put down what was left on the Princess. That's why I needed a partner, to buy the fixtures and inventory. What do you think of her?"

My eyes were adjusting to the dusty light coming in through the windows. The room was larger and simpler than the Orient in Socorro City, with wood chips on the plank floor and the standard lithographs razored out of eastern publications and framed on the walls, racehorses and boxers. The bar itself was plain pine and lacked a rail. The mirror behind it was a giveaway, carrying an advertisement for the Hermitage Distillery of Franklin County, Kentucky, dressed up a little with red-white-and-blue bunting. There were eight tables, including a faro layout in the corner, and three hurricane lamps swinging from the ceiling.

"Who supplies the stock?" I asked.

"Distributor in El Paso. We're on the route. That bar's temporary. I put in a bid on a honey in El Paso del Norte across the border. Mexico City closed the place down for treating with enemies of the republic. This here's Irish Andy. He won't tell me his other name. I hired him right out from under the Mare's Nest down the street."

I shook hands with the man behind the bar, blue eyes and a sheared head on a buffalo neck with shoulders to match, aproned from his neck to his knees. He had one of those fixed smiles you wanted to trust but knew better. I asked him what part of Ireland he was from.

"Frankfurt." His accent was as thick as a Prussian lance. "What can I pour you?"

"Bet you could eat the asshole out of a skunk," Junior put in. "We got a stove in back."

"I'll have a steak and a bottle."

Andy stood a bottle and a glass on the bar and went through the curtain in back. Junior and I sat down at a table out of the sunlight. He folded his blue-veined hands on the table and watched me drink. "Ever throw a lip over any whiskey smoother than that?" Liquid eyes pleaded.

"I've had loads worse. I guess you still can't drink hard liquor."

"Ties my guts in square knots." He kneaded his hands. "Page, I'm sore glad you came in with me. To tell you the truth I never thought you would when I wrote you. I figured after all this time you had that star tattooed on."

"Six years is as long as I do anything. I was grateful you kept the offer open. It took me three months to make up my mind."

"You pulled me out of more than one bog. I calculated I owed you that much time and then some." He chewed the ends of the moustaches he'd been nurturing for as long as I'd known him. They disappeared in strong light. "Shit, whose hind leg am I pulling? The Lord's truth is I didn't have no other takers."

The thing that had sunk in me when I got my first look at the town sank again. "You swore to me it was a sound investment."

"Oh, the Princess is a hell of a lot more than just that. We got the Butterfield coming through four times a month and there's talk the Atchison might run a spur out here, and until then we have those trail herders stealing Mexican beef, which is thirsty work. I just don't inspire confidence. Folks that don't know me look at me and think I am bound to crumple under the first hard rain."

"They don't know you for certain."

"Well, there you have it. I was thinking of selling out to Eille MacNutt at the Mare's Nest when the wire came with your end. That money came in handy, I can tell you."

A whiff of hot grease reached my nostrils from in back. My stomach started to gnaw. I poured whiskey into it. "When's the next herd come through? It's been a long time since I played with house money. I need to practice."

"That's the other thing. You won't be the only one playing with house money."

"You hired a dealer?"

"No. No, not exactly." He looked down at his hands.

I stuck the cork back in the bottle. "Who'd you cut in and for how much?"

"Now, Page, I had expenses. The carpenter I hired never done a roof before. It leaked and I had to bring in somebody else to do it right. Lumber's dear. The wholesale price of whiskey went up. Then the note came due on the town lot. There was other things. It's all in the ledger." He pried his hands apart and laid them palms down. "It was a third interest."

"You sold half of my half without telling me?"

"You'll get your end."

"It isn't that I'm concerned about. I came all this way thinking I owned fifty percent of something and now I find out I'm part of a syndicate. We had a deal, Junior."

"You want out?"

"What if I said yes? That ruby stickpin wouldn't bring today's interest on what you owe me."

"I'll go back to ranch work if I need to. My old man would pay you your time in the middle of a stampede if you asked, and I am his son. If it takes twenty years I'll settle the debt."

"Hell." I took the cork back out and refilled my glass. "For all we know they won't even honor cash money come the new century. Sheep will be the coin of the union. That or silk hats."

"Does that mean you're still in?"

"Ask me again after I meet our new partner."

"That will be Friday when the stage comes in. I won't tell you any names until then. You're ripe for a surprise, partner. Eille MacNutt too, though not one so pleasant. He has the notion that string of whores of his makes him king of the alkali flat."

"I won't run whores," I warned him. "Keeping the peace for Judge Blackthorne is as low as I've crawled or ever plan to."

"Whores are trouble I don't require. You feed them and put clothes on their backs and pay the doctor when they catch a cold in their pantaloons and then they run off and marry the first drunk cowboy who asks. I say let them get drunk here and take their proposals down the street."

My steak came, trailing black smoke off a blue china plate. It crunched like hardtack when I chewed, but I finished it and washed it down with whiskey. Not counting a pemmican cake at my cold camp the night before, my last meal had been a tortilla and chili peppers in Socorro City; a mistake, as I'd found out after two hours on the trail.

I pushed away the empty plate. "I feel I should explain this Satan's Sixgun business."

"I always heard he carried a pitchfork."

There was no irony in his expression. The phrase meant nothing to him. I felt my face grinning. "I may just take to this place after all."

"It grows on you. It does for a fact."

"I didn't see a hotel or a boardinghouse on my way in. Where do I sleep?"

"Your room's over the faro game, thought you'd appreciate that. Mine's over the bar. The stairs are outside. I guess you want to put up your boots."

"After I visit the bathhouse. Also the marshal's office. The sheriff says I have to register there."

"The son of a bitch. I don't know which is worse for business, him, his brother, or the Apaches. At least the savages don't smile at you when they're cutting your balls off."

"He claims Ross is dead."

"That's horseshit. He stays below the border where the American authorities can't arrest him and plans robberies of pack trains from the mines. Does a little rustling too, but that's practically legal around here. After each silver robbery Frank sends out posses in every direction but the right one. Them James boys up in Missouri could learn something from watching the Baronets."

I changed the subject. "What kind of man is the town marshal?"

His face lightened. "Oh, you have a treat coming

in Rosario Ortiz. He is the biggest thing to hit this place since Billy the Kid shot the blacksmith."

We talked for a little while longer and then I went up to drop off my things in my new quarters. I was thinking that just a few days ago I had never heard of Billy the Kid, and now I was sick of the name.

# ⤳ 5 ⤶

THE COMBINATION BARBERSHOP and bathhouse that couldn't make up its mind whether to stay adobe or go wooden was just as undecided inside. There was a clear joint where the new tongue-and-groove floorboards met the old worn planks with cracks between them into which a careless barber could sweep ears and things, and someone had tacked up tent material to keep out the weather where the original mud wall didn't quite bunt up against the fresh studs. The proprietor was a small dour Mexican who scraped my face with half a dozen expert strokes. Mexicans are generally good with razors and don't bore you with conversation.

The room I returned to from the shave and a bath was clean and smelled of sawdust. It had a clothespress, a basin, a bed with a feather mattress, and a lantern on a nail. The inevitable Indian rug lay on the floor waiting to deaden the noise from downstairs, of which there was none at that hour of the afternoon. The soft enveloping mattress was a poor choice for the climate, but I stripped to the skin and slept two hours without interruption. Instant oblivion, in my late line of work, was a prize you either won or failed to acquire and learned to function at half your natural capacity three quarters of the time.

I put on my town clothes and stepped out under a rusty sky to present myself to the local law. I didn't look west. The color spectacle would go on for the best part of an hour, and I had seen enough of them lately to last my life. I would have to stop missing the sudden sunsets in the Bitterroots before I called this place home.

The building I had been directed to by Junior Harper stood at the north end of town on the other side of a plank bridge over a dry riverbed, inconvenient to everything but the ancient mission in whose shadow it spent twelve hours of every day. It was small, adobe of course, built in the old Spanish style without brick reinforcing, and patched many times with mud and clay that dried to varying shades, its roof poles extending two feet into the desert air for the purpose of stringing up hides and reluctant Roman Catholics. The stick door hung as crooked as an Indian agent.

A fat Mexican in overalls and a cavalry coat, so stained and weather-faded I couldn't tell which army it had belonged to, knelt in a strip of loam protected by rocks next to the door, probing for feathergrass roots with a bayonet that had seen all its glory days and cursing softly in that bastard border dialect you heard all over that territory. A snaggle of yellow roses that were more thorn than blossom appeared to be the beneficiaries of all this industry. They hardly seemed worth it, but then I had seen a man lose his life defending his wife's imported china from a group of drunken buffalo hunters in a restaurant in Cheyenne. In a land of spines and diamondbacks some men will go to any length on behalf of beauty.

"Marshal's office," I said.

The Mexican started, shielded his eyes up at me, and stood, snatching off his sombrero. His gray hair was cut in a bowl and his handlebars, untrimmed and tobacco-stained at the ends, underscored a twentyweight of pockmarked jowls. His nose was the size of an avocado.

"*Allá, mi jefe.*" He gestured toward the door with the sombrero. "In there."

"*Gracias.*" I pulled the latchstring. The door flopped open.

As soon as I was inside I knew the Mexican had misunderstood my question. It was a house like a thousand others in and around old Mexico, decorated with bunches of dried chili peppers hung from the ceiling and straw pallets on the dirt floor. There was a dugout fireplace with a trivet for cooking, a square plank table stained all over and scored many times by knives used to slice meat and tortillas, and on the other side of it a piano stool that had been rescued from a wagon trail or some white family's trash, discharging horsehair out of its burst seat. A naked child no older than two sat there trying to spin itself sick. The little house, in fact, was filled with children of every age and both sexes, all of them engaged in something destructive that required noise. One, a boy of about six, had discovered that the back wall had a timber frame and was busy chipping away adobe with a carving knife to expose it further. The din was enough to make you yearn for the serenity of a slaughterhouse in St. Louis.

I was turning to leave when the fat Mexican stepped past me and barked a single syllable that knocked dust out of a rafter. It was like the last shot at Appomattox. The children stopped what they were doing and turned as one to stare at the entrant with large dark shiny eyes like wet olive pits. He strode through the silence, accumulating authority as he went, and paused by the table.

"Josefina."

This time he spoke gently. The naked child slid off the stool and scampered around behind him, peering out at me as from the cover of a post. He shooed it away with a pat on its split behind, straddled the stool with a grunt and a sigh, and fished inside first one, then the other side pocket of the cavalry coat until he came up with a bent star and hung it on the tobacco pocket in front.

"*Buenas tardes, señor,*" he said. "What can I do for you this day?"

"You're the marshal?"

"*Sí,* part of the time. By trade I am a master carpenter. I am called Rosario Ortiz." He didn't offer to shake hands. His were filthy from the flower bed.

"Page Murdock." There was no reaction. "I'm new part owner of the Apache Princess."

He smiled with all his teeth. It was like a sunburst. "The Princess, *sí.* I do the roof right. The other fellow, he makes privies." Suddenly he stopped smiling.

"The roof has a leak? I fix it for free. Ortiz stands behind his work."

"I'm sure it's fine. I've come to register."

"Register?" He blinked. "Oh, *sí, sí*. Yes. By order of the sheriff." He looked around, including under the table, lifted his sombrero off the top and put it down. Finally he shot a stream of Spanish at one of the children, a grave-faced boy of fourteen or fifteen, who said, "*Sí,* Papa," and went out the open door at the back.

"I apologize for my worthless children."

"I've seen worse," I said, "though not so many in one place."

The boy returned carrying a green ledger stuffed with loose pages. Ortiz spread it open carefully and leafed through it until he came to the page he wanted. He went through the ritual search once more and said something to another child, a girl this time who had begun to develop breasts under her white cotton shift. She went to a painted cabinet with a bucket on top, opened a door, and came over to the table with a horsehair pen and a bottle of purple ink. He unstopped the bottle, dipped the pen, and turned the ledger to face me, holding the pen out.

"Your signature please, *Señor* Murdock. Your mark will be sufficient if you cannot write."

I accepted the pen and scratched my name between ruled lines. There were only two others on the page: Ford Harper, Jr. and Eille MacNutt. Someone had neatly printed MacNutt's name next to a ragged *X*. I handed back the pen.

"The registration fee is five dollars."

I whistled. The marshal looked apologetic. "I keep not a penny, *señor*. It all goes to the county seat."

"The county seat being Frank Baronet's faro bank." I flipped a gold piece onto the table. It bounced and he caught it against his chest. He bit down on it, studied the result, and entered the transaction next to my signature.

"A carpenter can work anywhere, and I do not care to keep the peace," he said. "I would leave, but my wife is buried behind the mission."

"I'm sorry."

"It is not your sorrow. I am the one who shot her."

He placed the coin inside the ledger, closed it, and returned the star to his side pocket. Rising and giving me a slight bow, he set the sombrero on his head and went out to tend his roses. As soon as he crossed the threshold the children resumed their loud destructive activities.

The faro equipment at the Apache Princess was strictly basic. The layout was an oilcloth with the card denominations crudely painted on it and there was no cue box. Instead the dealer was obliged to keep a running tally of the cards dealt with a pencil and paper or by transferring chips from one stack to another with each deal. The cards were worn and the painted tiger on the card box had had so many thumbs run across it the stripes were all rubbed off. I played three miners, slab-faced failed farmers in flannel shirts beaten clean on rocks, traces of black clay crusted behind their ears, but they all left before I could get a rhythm going either way. Even the one that quit ahead looked as glum as if he'd lost his grubstake. Junior, who had been tending bar while Irish Andy ate his supper in back, flipped him the towel and came over and sat down. "Odds against the house tonight?"

"Who could blame them? I saw fresher decks in Leadville, where they threw the slops in the street."

"I have a trimmer here somewhere."

"I arrested a man once for shooting a man for owning a card trimmer. Some places that's all the evidence they need to lynch you."

"I never heard evidence was required. Anyway, not everyone uses them to shave cards, just to tidy up the fuzzy edges. New decks are expensive out here, especially when you order them by the case. Who cares if the jack of diamonds has a clean collar?"

"Let me ask you this." I dealt us each a hand of poker. "What makes a cowboy come to a place like this and gamble?"

"That's an easy one, to win money. Two." He discarded two pasteboards from his hand. I replaced them and stood pat.

"Wrong. He can do that back at the bunkhouse without having to put on a clean shirt. What makes that same cowboy come to a saloon and pay for his whiskey by the glass when he can buy a bottle for less and drink it at home?"

"You're the one making the point. What are we playing for?"

"Education."

"In that case I call."

I turned over four sixes. He threw his hand into the deadwood. "Deal another."

I shuffled and dealt. "He comes here for the noise and colors and things going on. Music, if there's any, but there doesn't have to be. Other men and loud talk and the naked lady on the couch in the picture over the bar. Something he doesn't have at home. Dealer takes one." He did the same. "Gambling's no different," I went on. "He likes to hear the counters click and slide his fingers over the wax on the cards and he wants that tiger on the box to look so real it might take his arm off if he bets wrong. Call."

He laid his cards face up. He had a ten-high straight. I showed him a heart flush.

"One thing he don't want." Junior sat back. "He don't want them cards coming off the wrong end of the deck. If you're fixing to keep on doing that in here, you best get a whole lot better at it fast. John Whiteside's hands will sew you up in a green hide and leave you out in the sun to cogitate on your sins."

"I only cheat when it doesn't count. How about a new layout?"

"I have the catalogue. Pick out what you want and we'll order it. No billiard tables, mind. You will find all you need strung out along the Jornada del Muerto, complete with the bones of the wagoneers that tried to slide them past the Apaches. Those killers have got a Philadelphia Ladies League mad on against that game. Old Cochise must have had him a snookering." He watched me laying out a hand of patience. "Did you make the acquaintance of our local James Butler Hickok?"

"Oh, Marshal Ortiz and I are old friends. He showed me his children and his roses."

"Ten years from now those kids are going to make Quantrill's raiders look like *East Lynne*. We had the frame up on a schoolhouse when two of them burned it down. Almost wiped out San Sábado. Rosario only has the job because he will work for found. Did he tell you he killed his wife?"

"It came up during the conversation."

"It generally does. It's the only thing ever happened to him worth talking about. Story I heard when I came was he caught her on the floor between pews in the mission with a Yaquí mine worker, missed him, and shot her clean to hell. Personally I think he done it by accident while seating a charge in that old ball-and-percussion pistol he uses to shoot stray dogs and coyotes. If them kids can't get him mad enough to beat the devil out of them I don't see how his wife could do it just by misplacing her vows."

"You never married, I guess."

"Did you?"

"I thought about it. I can see how it could make you mad enough."

"Hell, yes, *you*. Not Ortiz."

I placed a red deuce on a black trey. "Did he soak you five dollars when you registered?"

He nodded. "Eille MacNutt too, and a dollar for every whore besides. Our sheriff must have enough to retire on registration fees alone, when you figure in all the saloons and sporting houses in the county. Then there's the percentage he gets for collecting taxes."

"That's a job of work. Cattlemen are a rough cob when it comes to paying their fair share."

"Not when you have an assassin like that deputy of his siding you," he said.

"Jubilo? He didn't strike me as the kind."

"Nobody knows a Mexican but another Mexican. The talk is a firing squad's waiting for him across the border. Then there was that business up in Lincoln with both Baronets. Ross or Frank killed this poor dumb rancher, but they say Jubilo done for the wife. Spooner, their name was. Dave and Vespa. Shot dead in front of their own house."

"I heard Frank might not have been in on that."

"Ross never done a thing that Frank didn't know about it. If he wasn't there you can be damn sure he told Ross where to put the slugs. All them Spooners done wrong was to side with Chisum against Dolan and Murphy. I guess they were what you would call an example."

"The sheriff seems to favor those." I touched the swelling along my temple where he'd laid the barrel of his Remington.

"Frank done that? I noticed but I didn't want to ask. What did you do that stirred him up?"

"Not much. I threatened to kill a stable hand."

He grinned and shook his head. "I swear, Page, you always did draw fire. I remember that time in Missoula—"

"So do I." I went bust and gathered up the cards. "I sure do shine at picking a spot to settle down."

## 6

I WASN'T IN town Friday when the stage came in from El Paso. A saloon is a low place to be mornings, with sunlight lying on the cheap stain that passes for elegant mahogany at night and the human debris hunched in the corners over the first glass of the day with their buttons all undone because their hands are shaking too hard to fasten them. No one is gambling, at least not with anything as meaningless and as much fun as money. I put on my trail clothes and rode out for some target practice in the bright blue open. The trigger pull of the Deane-Adams needed sweetening from time to time and so did my aim. Marshaling wasn't the only profession that required those things up to the mark. There were a lot of bad gamblers out there who weren't aware that money was meaningless and as much fun to lose as it was to win.

The claybank liked the snappy cold of a desert

morning, arching its long neck and cocking its legs high as if running involved less effort than standing still. I tethered it to a low piñon tree and walked away fifty yards to pot at stones and elbows on branches, watching out the corner of my eye for its reaction to gunfire. It snapped up its head after the first shot, then reached back to bite an itch. John Whiteside, who had fought Indians and Mexicans and Johnny Rebs both on foot and from horseback, had trained it well.

The coach driver, around thirty with a full beard and that facial twitch you saw often in men who spent much of their time trying to keep arrowheads and bandits' bullets out of their backs, was checking the team for fistulas in front of the freight office when I returned. I saw that rather than waste one of his pretty Concords on a flyspeck like San Sábado, Mr. Butterfield had sent a common mud wagon, open on both sides with only canvas flaps between passengers and the weather. The seats were empty now and the luggage gone.

I found Junior conferring with the cedar chief in front of the Apache Princess, smoking a tailor-made with ladylike puffs to avoid drawing smoke too far into his finely balanced system. The day was warming up but he still wore a sheepskin over his frock coat and vest and a wideawake hat that made him look like something stunted in the shade of the great brim. "Our partner got in an hour ago and is waiting for us at *Señora* Castillo's boardinghouse," he said. "The *señora* is one of our celebrated widows. Ugly as a washboard and cooks like one, but it's the only place to stay in town until we get a hotel built. I didn't know we'd need another room when I put up this place."

"Who is he, Jay Gould? Why can't he meet us here?"

"You saw the stage. Would you feel like walking this distance once you finished scrubbing off New Mexico?"

"This rig okay to meet him in, or do I need a morning coat?"

"Let's go. You are the complainingest partner."

The house was on an alley off the main street and was probably the oldest wooden building in town, built of barked logs with the chinking as thick in places as a man's wrist. *Señora* Castillo, older yet, greeted us at the door holding a straw broom in the fashion of a weapon. She was as dark and wrinkled as a chili pepper and bent nearly double in a coarse black dress with a dusty hem and hundreds of black bead buttons up the front. A plain gray scarf completely covered her hair. No eyes showed in the black crescent hollows between the puckered lids. I had seen more life in Aztec masks. When Junior told her what we were about she turned and led the way inside, dragging both feet with a sound like a locomotive champing at the platform.

The parlor was a combination of Mexican and Chicago Victorian. Oval portraits of bitter-faced men in whiskers hung on the log walls, a serape covered most of the worn spots on an overstuffed sofa, a tea table with yellow pottery on it stood on an earthen floor swept as bare as tile. The place smelled of extinct meals and dry rot.

"Good morning, Marshal. I suppose it is Mr. Murdock now."

I stopped, letting Junior walk past me to the middle of the room. The voice coming from the direction of the sofa was husky for a woman, slightly roughened from years of calling for wagers in smoky barrooms full of loud men in a fever to lose their gold dust and coppers. She had aged some—her cheekbones were more pronounced and there was a vertical crease where before there had been only white forehead as smooth as glaze—but her hair, done up loosely, was still Indian black and the eyes, set just a shade too wide, were clear blue with tiny gold points floating in them like snowflakes in a crystal paperweight. The mouth was excessive too for fashion but well formed, the chin cut delicately but firm. Her dress was cambric, plain white and cut simply to her clean figure and closed at the throat with an amber brooch set in rose gold. The contrast with her black patent leather high-tops, and with the dark colors that surrounded her, was marked. But then I knew from old experience that it was her business to stand out.

"Just Murdock will serve," I said. "Is it still Mrs. Bower, or have you gone back to Poker Annie?"

"I never went by it. That was a mistake on a circular that went out in Dakota and it stuck. The circular was a mistake as well. I see you are as sweet-natured as ever."

"Mrs. Colleen Bower, Page Murdock," Junior said. "The old man always insisted I was born a day late and managed to fall behind an hour a year. I had a notion you two were old acquaintances. It had to be more than just your reputation that almost backed Mrs. Bower out of the deal when your name came up."

She had been dabbing at her throat with a lace handkerchief when we entered, blotting the moisture that surfaced in the dry heat through pores freshly open from the bath. Now she returned the pretty to the reticule in her lap, white satin with a black drawstring. "Breen, Montana, is a ghost city now. Lumber rats got the boards after the cattle interests pulled out, leaving just the foundations and broken glass where the saloons were. Two years ago it was wide open and filled with desperate men. Mr. Murdock held his own."

"Mrs. Bower is a fair judge of that breed. She's known so many."

"That's small even for a killer."

I pointed my chin at the purse. "Do you still carry that pocket pistol in your bag, or have you stitched the holster to your petticoat by now?"

Junior interrupted. "A gentleman never discusses underwear with a lady. Anyway we are here to talk business. Sundays are for reminiscing."

"Sit, Mr. Murdock. I assume you still bend far enough for that."

I thought about answering. Instead I stepped past a walnut rocker and pulled up a ladder-back that someone had promoted from the trash pile and put back into use with splints and buckhide thongs. A thousand acres of dust had settled since the last time I had wanted to be comfortable in Colleen Bower's company.

"Now we are all friends." Junior perched on the opposite end of the sofa, placing his hat in his lap. "Let's not show off our Spanish, by the by. The old hag has ears like a bat." *Señora* Castillo had removed herself through a doorway behind a hanging shawl.

"I will come to the point. As I recall, you favor that approach over all the others." Flecked blue eyes fixed me. "As Junior said, when we met in El Paso and he told me you were involved I considered withholding my end. However, my situation there was hardly an improvement."

I nodded. "Poke Allyard was marshal there last I heard. He isn't the kind to be gotten around with paint and scent like the late peace officer of Breen."

"The circuit is a cruel enough place for a man. Try being a woman and see if you don't employ what God gave you to keep you in biscuits and sardines. To continue. This is a business relationship as Junior pointed out. Men are finding silver all over this country and the butchers in Chicago are standing by the U.P. tracks with their knives out just waiting for that cheap Mexican beef. El Paso—"

"Cheap meaning stole," Junior said.

" 'Every great fortune begins with a crime.' Balzac." She kept looking at me. "El Paso is too far for these cowboys and miners to go to spend their money on cards and liquor. There are too many Apaches on the way to Socorro City and a bandit behind every piñon tree between here and old Mexico. San Sábado promises to become the next Tombstone. I'm certain you know what that signifies."

"For starters I'm happy it's not my job to keep the

peace. All the news I hear from Tombstone has hair and fangs."

"A fine peace you kept in Breen."

"It got kept. I didn't seek the post. Your benefactor strangled on a piece of gristle and Judge Blackthorne appointed me."

"Beside the point. I should not have brought it up. What I am driving at is people are making their fortunes in Tombstone. We could make ours here if we will only forget the back trail and pull together between the traces."

"I have nothing against making a fortune."

"Then perhaps we should start by shaking hands." She offered me one of hers.

I let out air and took it. It was as cool and smooth as I remembered, all except the small callosities on the fingertips from handling pasteboards and chips. She had been clutching her reticule with it, and when she changed hands I admired the plain band on the third finger of the left. I knew her as a self-made widow who didn't wear one. "I guess good wishes are in order."

"Thank you." She withdrew her right and placed it on top of the other, covering the ring. "Now that we have smoked the peace pipe, you can settle a point. For weeks now Junior and I have been burning up the wires arguing over whether the Apache Princess should be renovated. I hold that it should."

"Why renovated? It's only just built."

"That's what I said." Junior pushed the dents out of the wideawake's crown and put them back in.

"You and I and Junior Harper are not the only people on the frontier with vision," she said. "Once we begin separating these miners and cowboys from their pokes, just how long do you think it will be before this town has more saloons than widows? If we are going to draw more than just a grubstake to start over somewhere else when the others crowd us out, we must plan to meet the competition now. Junior informs me that you are adamant about not keeping whores."

"I am."

"He holds the opinion that my presence alone will draw customers away from the women at the Mare's Nest."

I looked at him. "You said that?"

"Not first thing," he said. "They will all want their turn, women of easy virtue being an improvement over a knothole in the side of a buckboard, if you'll disregard my coarse language, ma'am." He'd have tipped his hat if he were wearing it. "My guess is you haven't seen the Mare's Nest women yet."

"That bad?"

"Coyote girls, the lot. You know, when you wake up to find one laying on your arm and you chew it off to get away. Once they have all had their turn they will come here to look at something that reminds them of a female. Don't forget these are men who will ride forty miles to see a picture of Lillie Langtry. All the renovation we require is to paint 'Poker Annie' in big yellow letters under the Cold Beer sign and they will bet on there being fifty-three cards in a standard deck just for the opportunity to sit across the table from Mrs. Bower and tell their friends about it back in camp."

I grinned. "Junior, how is it no one sold you the

governor's palace in Santa Fe on your way down here?"

He looked blank. "I came by way of El Paso."

Colleen reached across the sofa to pat his knee. "You're a ring-tailed dreamer and that's why I took you up on your proposition and came here. Boom-towns attract good-looking women. In six months I will look like *Señora* Castillo next to some of them. Ask Murdock."

"That's true enough. They follow the market."

"Lumber is cheap now," she said. "We need to expand, build a gaming room in back. That will allow more than just faro and poker and free up space here for more drinking and a stage. I know a theatrical agent in Saint Louis who can supply talent, singers and tumblers and Shakespearean companies. It would surprise you to learn how starved these illiterate tinpans are for *Troilus and Cressida*. Next month they are auctioning off the fixtures at the Crystal Palace in El Paso. The owner shot himself over a marital misunderstanding and his widow needs cash. We can pick up a hickory bar and brass pulls and a chandelier with gimcrackery and doodads. Items like those are bound to impress the rubes clean out of their overalls and everything in the pockets. People will read about the Apache Princess in Boston."

"I have a line on a bar." Junior was petulant.

"What will we use to acquire all this elegance, besides a six-shooter?" I asked.

"We can borrow the money and offer the saloon as collateral."

Junior bared his teeth. "Borrow from who, Geronimo? The nearest bank with that kind of capital is in Santa Fe and it won't gamble on anything this close to the border. It's the first place I went when I decided to become a saloonkeeper."

"There has to be someone in the vicinity with means and the itch to increase them. A rancher."

He shook his head. "That'd be John Whiteside, but everything he has is tied up in cattle. I doubt he would invest in an enterprise in town anyway."

"Frank Baronet."

Four eyes met mine. Junior's treadle-shaped jaw fell open. "That diamondback son of a bitch? Your pardon," he said to Colleen.

But she wasn't listening. "Who is he? Does he have money?"

I told her who he was. "Sheriffing is a porkbarrel job out here. He gets to claim a percentage of the taxes he collects, and the registration fees and what-not he imposes by his own order probably go into his personal war chest. On top of that he has the gaming concession at the Orient in Socorro City and who knows how large a piece of how many others. It's his county, he answers to no one but the governor, and he doesn't answer to this governor. Then his brother is a desperado, a dead one officially but alive probably, and successful. Brothers share. Yes, I would say he has money."

"You don't make him sound like a friend. Would he be interested in investing?"

"I've only known him a short time. With some people that's all you need. My impression is if this place has as much potential as you say, he'll find a way to cut himself in even if we don't invite him. Especially if we don't. This way at least we'd have some of his money to play with."

"And his hand in our pocket till Gabriel blows." Junior stood and tugged on his hat. "You know my position. The notion of cutting Frank Baronet in as a fourth partner don't sweeten the tea."

"That's one vote. Murdock?"

"I've sided worse. At least we can trust Baronet to deal us dirt if he sees the chance. It's the not being sure that makes most arrangements go south."

"Call that a vote yes. Carried. We'll discuss the details tonight. I'm dealing."

I was looking down at her now. "Friday is the first good night of the week. I might have known you'd claim it."

"The Princess has more than one table, and I have my own board and cue box. Deal or don't." She lifted a book off the arm of the sofa and opened it. The title on the pebbled cover read *The Gentleman's Guide to Percentages in Games of Chance.*

Outside, Junior asked, "Are you really fixing to climb into bed with Baronet after what he done to you in Socorro City?"

"That was personal. This is business. The protection of his office is worth something. Anyway he'll nickel and dime us to death if we don't."

"I'm opposed to it." Suddenly he grinned; his disposition had more varieties than the weather in Montana. "I thought for a minute there you and Colleen was going for your irons."

"I wish you'd told me she was the partner."

"Swear to God, you spend a winter with a man in

a line shack you think you know him. I never suspected."

"Suspected what?"

"That you could fall in love so hard."

## 7

AS IT HAPPENED, Colleen Bower and I didn't have the chance to discuss renovations that night. Early on the gamblers were stacked six deep at her table to play and watch, and later I had to kill a man, which makes concentration difficult.

I dealt a few hands of faro and finished ahead, no slight accomplishment when you consider it's the serious ones who keep track of the cards who will sit at a man's table when someone like Poker Annie is dealing in the corner. Tonight she had a silver comb in her hair and a red silk choker around her neck that just naturally drew the eyes down the front of her dress, which was some kind of layered thing of lace and percale that made you think it was cut lower than it was, anchored at the shoulders by two simple bows. It was a rare bettor who could pay attention to the pasteboards when it looked like one of those bows would work loose any second, spilling her femaleness out over the table. Men have no understanding of costume architecture.

About ten o'clock I ran out of dedicated players and went to spell Irish Andy behind the bar. You couldn't have pounded a shim between customers there and for half an hour Junior and I were too busy washing and filling glasses to talk. When at last there was a lull he mopped his face and slung the towel over his shoulder. "I always wanted a job with a collar," he said. "I never thought I'd be sweating into it so much. I might as well be roping and throwing."

"This pays better and doesn't smell as bad. How are we doing?"

"Not as well as she is. What do you suppose it is makes a man bet so foolish with a woman he can't even have?"

"Judge Blackstone told me once there's no desert harder to cross than the two feet that separate a man's brain from his penis. He was hanging a man for rape at the time."

"It ain't my business asking what soured you on her."

I drew a beer for a miner at the end of the bar, sliding it down the side of the glass to cut down on foam, and skidded it into his hand. "She is too much cards for me. There were three sides to take in Breen and she laid side bets with all of them. If I lived she won. If I got killed she won too. A situation like that is hard on a man's good opinion of himself."

"Might could be you were expecting too much."

"No might-coulds about it," I said. "But I won't compound the mistake by repeating it."

"I don't know. Some of my best mistakes was made on the second run. How's the keg?"

I pulled the bung-starter out of its socket next to the sawed-off and gave the beer keg a couple of raps. "Better have one ready."

"First one generally lasts past eleven on Friday. You have to stop being so generous, running the beer down the glass that way. We charge the same for air."

I was putting away the starter when three fresh customers came through the flap door. Trouble clung to them like wolf scent.

Men had been coming in and going out, but when they arrived in a bunch they either stayed together or split between the bar and Colleen's table. This crew peeled off in three directions. One, puny and consumptive-looking in a duster snagged with nettles and a miner's cap made of greasy ticking, went straight to the table without pausing. Another, larger and bulkier in a slouch hat and a hide coat too heavy for the weather, stepped to the side wall and placed his back against it, the one spot in the room that yielded an unobstructed view of the tables, the bar, and the door to the street.

The third didn't look like he belonged with the first two. The shortest of the three and stocky, he wore a corduroy shooting coat with leather patches, a black plug hat with a feather in the band, and a cartridge belt slantwise across his chest loaded with rifle shells belonging to the .45-70 Springfield drooping lazily in his left hand. There was something about the set of the bones in his face, with its neat beard and swooping moustaches, that reminded me of someone, but that wasn't the thing about him so much as the way he took in the room, rotating his head without moving his eyes, and the easy unhurried way he stationed himself at the door, looking as if he had just stopped there to search for a familiar face.

I figured he was the one with the orders, but it was the man in the hide coat with his back to the wall I chose to favor. Any heavy wrap worn out of season is likely to conceal something you'd rather not have exposed. While I groped for the shotgun the man by the table tugged an 1860 Army Colt with a Theur conversion out from under his duster and pointed it at Colleen Bower's head, crackling back the hammer in the same motion.

"Lay back or she gets it."

This from the man in the hide coat, who took advantage of my instant's hesitation to bring up a full-length Greener with both barrels already cocked. At that range the Apache Princess stood to lose two part owners, a number of paying customers, and several feet of bar. I laid back.

The room was quiet, painfully so after the rumble of male voices and thump and rustle of human activity that had been constant since just after sundown. Colleen was motionless behind her cue box.

"You." Hide Coat gestured at Junior with the Greener. "Put the cash box on the bar and slide it down towards the door."

Junior hung on a second, then lifted the tin Beacham's bread box into which he'd been stuffing notes and cartwheels all night off the shelf under the bar and placed it on top. It turned a little after he pushed it, upsetting a shot glass and splashing the lanky young cowboy whose drink it was. He did nothing.

The box now was within reach of the man with the Springfield but he made no move to pick it up.

Duster spoke for the first time. His speech was a shrill twang, the opposite end of the scale from Hide Coat's half-humorous baritone. "Now you, honey. Toss over that purse."

It was the white leather reticule, resting in her lap. Something might have fluttered over her face as she reached for it, the shadow of the reflection of the ghost of a smile, but then I was a gambler too and I noticed those things.

Irish Andy chose just that moment to come in from the back.

His close-cropped head was tilted down and he was tying his apron as he walked, unaware as yet of the silence in the room and what it signified. Hide Coat, startled by the sudden development, jerked his shotgun in that direction. I swung up the sawed-off, backing up a step to clear the top of the bar, and squeezed the rear trigger. Colleen fired at the same time but I didn't look for the result. Hide Coat was off his feet and headed for the wall backward, propelled by a pattern of buckshot as solid as a croquet ball, when I swung the second barrel on the man with the rifle, my finger wrapping the front trigger.

He was braced for a hipshot, both hands on the Springfield steadied alongside his pelvis with the hammer back. I saw him calculate the odds in an instant, a single rifle ball against shotgun spray, and I watched his muscles relax. Then he raised a palm in a brown jersey glove with the fingers cut out and backed away through the door.

*"Du lieber Gött."* Irish Andy goggled, his hands still behind him on his apron strings.

Junior was the first to move. As he strode to the end of the bar to rescue the cash box the tension broke apart in two halves. Voices and creaking floorboards came through the space between.

"Jesus. Christ Jesus."

Duster was still standing by the faro table, bent over now with his hands pinned between his knees. A pattern of fresh dark circles kept changing and growing on the floor between his feet and I couldn't tell which hand was hit. His Army Colt lay under the table. Colleen's bag rested on the table with her hand inside, smoldering from the powder flare of her pocket pistol.

Hide Coat was still alive and squirming in a muck of blood and sawdust on the floor, making wet sounds. I couldn't tell how much of his midsection remained beneath the mess I'd made of the hide. I came around the bar and stooped to pick up the Greener. I knew of two lawmen who'd been killed by men already dead for neglect of that chore.

The flap door opened. I swung that way, a shotgun in each hand. Rosario Ortiz stumbled in pulled by the weight of a Walker Colt as long as his forearm, a cap-and-ball model designed to ride in saddle scabbards and anchor rowboats. He had traded his overalls and cavalry tunic for a gray suit buttoned at the top of the coat and vest and nowhere else. His white-shirted belly hung out almost beyond the brim of his sombrero. The bent star sagged from the buttonhole in his lapel like one of his yellow roses.

"Hell's fire, Marshal, don't shoot one of us!" Junior stood cradling the bread tin in both arms.

All the customers were eager to report what had happened. I left them to it and went over to retrieve the Army pistol from under Colleen's table. The man in the duster had found a chair and sat in it now rocking to and fro, supporting his dripping right hand with his left and finding Jesus with every other breath.

"I understand Bill Cody is hiring precision shooters for his exhibition," I told Colleen. "You will need to practice some before you can pluck a half-dollar from between a man's fingers."

"I hadn't the luxury of taking aim. I wanted to hit the thickest part of him, but he hadn't any." She was frowning at the ruined reticule. "This one came from Monkey Ward's. I waited three months for delivery."

"It didn't go with that rig anyway."

Having established that there was no need for it, Marshal Ortiz threaded the long barrel of the Walker Colt inside the waistband of his trousers, obliging himself to walk stiff-legged as he made his rounds among the witnesses. You had to smile at the sight. That swift-draw thing was mostly an invention of novelists of the Jack Rimfire stamp, but a man could have eaten the free lunch in the time it would take the fat Mexican to bring that big pistol back out into the open. He listened to the accounts with his head bent, nodding energetically when he comprehended something and lifting his sombrero to scratch at his forelock with a black fingernail whenever some point differed from the others. Several times he crossed in front of the man dying on the floor, being careful each time to avoid treading in the blood with his boots, which were old-time Mexican cavalry issue worn round at the heels but blacked to a high shine on the toes. At length he stopped before the wounded robber in the chair and said something in a polite tone that was too low to make out from a distance of six feet.

"You go to hell, greaser."

Ortiz straightened with a sad look and came over to me. "I need your help, *señor.*"

"If you're deputizing me to ride with the posse I'm not interested," I said. "I left all that behind when I came south."

"Posse? No posse. I need assistance removing this man to the mission."

I wasn't sure which man he meant. "Why there? Can't the padre come here? I never heard where the Last Rites in a saloon didn't take."

"You misunderstand, *Señor* Murdock. San Sábado has no jail. When it is necessary to hold a man for the sheriff we use the mission cellar. It has a trapdoor. The old fathers and brothers hid women and children there from Indians in times past. The doctor can bind his hand here but I will require someone to help me get him down the ladder afterward. The shock, it makes a man weak."

"Can't someone take care of that while you go out after the third man?"

He scratched his forelock. "*¿Por qué?* Why? You have your money."

"That doesn't make what he did any less illegal."

"The only reason to chase a man at night is to get back what he has taken, no?"

"What's to stop him from trying again? We don't even know who he is."

"Oh, we know his name."

"We do?"

The toothy smile behind his handlebars was eager to please in a way that made me want to push it in. "I apologize, *señor*. I forget you are new. The man with the hole in his hand is Abel Freestone. The man you have killed is called Dutch Tim. Everyone in this country knows who they favor with their company."

I glanced toward the door the man with the Springfield had gone through. I remembered the vaguely familiar set of his features. "For a twin, Ross Baronet doesn't look that much like his brother, does he?"

"They are not, how do you say, identical."

"Like hell they're not," I said.

The man on the floor had stopped squirming.

## 8

THE BELL IN the mission tower began to bang out Mass a few minutes before seven Sunday morning. The sun wedging its way over the San Andres was pretty but the color reminded me of the corruption we'd had to scrape off the floor of the Princess Friday night. The planks would still need sanding and a fresh application of sawdust to remove Dutch Tim's final traces. As for the rest of him, I'd given five dollars to the little Mexican who sheared hair at the barbershop to scratch a hole in the cramped patch of unconsecrated ground east of town and erect a board. He doubled as town undertaker.

He weighed the gold piece on his palm. "A board for a bandit?"

"I want his friends to see what his line of work got him."

"You wish an inscription?"

I thought. " 'God's finger touched him and he slept.' "

"More like a full load of double-ought buck," said Junior when he heard about it.

That was Saturday morning. Now, after four hours' sleep on top of the Saturday night crush, I was in front of the Princess lashing my bedroll across the claybank's big rump. Junior came out yawning bitterly in his morning sheepskin and wideawake hat.

"You got a good day for it," he said, leaning against a porch post.

"Yes. I can cook my noon dinner on a rock without having to make a fire."

"Damn shame sending you back out into it. You just got here."

"No help for it. Your feelings about the sheriff are too strong to negotiate with him and I doubt Colleen's purse pistol shoots far enough to keep her out of some three-legged buck's wigwam."

"Baronet's bound to think Ross scared you into offering him a cut."

"I disagree. Ross is out two men because of us."

"Think he knew what Ross was up to?"

"Maybe. If he did he'll offer me special protection before I even bring up our proposition." I checked the magazine of the Winchester and scabbarded it.

"Here come *las viudas.*"

I turned in time to see the last of perhaps a dozen old women step off the boardwalk on the other side of the street and turn in the direction of the mission. They were dressed all in black from bonnets to shoes, their dark hems dragging like crows' wings in the dust of the street. One or two fingered rosaries; the rest clutched their shawls at the throat and stared straight ahead as they walked, moving with a kind of bicycling gait that raised a yellow plume in their wake. The group swept along like some low-hanging cloud and seemed to drain the life from everything it passed.

Junior said, "California has its swallows and we have our magpies. They gather at one or another's house at first light and go to Mass in a flock. That's how it's been every Sunday for as long as anyone can remember."

"I thought it was just some leftover legend. I didn't think the widows were real."

"In a few years they won't be. Eille MacNutt says when he came to town there was twice this many, and three times that many twenty years before that. This is what's left from the last vendetta. Any town that is running out of widows can't be all bad."

"I'd feel better if I didn't think someone probably said the same thing just before the last vendetta."

No sooner had he mentioned Eille MacNutt than two women came out the door of the Mare's Nest, tying on head scarves as they followed the widows. Their dresses were more subdued than what they would wear for work and cut for the parlor, but they seemed as bright as plumage against the group that had passed ahead of them.

"It's a sad day when a whore gets religion," said Junior. "Next comes married and babies and then the Wednesday League to stamp out the things that bring them here to begin with."

"That's civilization."

"Now you sound like the old man. And every time he said it he jacked the ranch house up on rails and moved it farther back toward the mountains." He

tipped his hat back with a knuckle. "If that's civilization, what do you call this here?"

I followed the slant of his chin. Another woman
had come to the corner from the side street that led to
*Señora* Castillo's boardinghouse, paused to check for
traffic, and turned in behind the women from the
Mare's Nest. She was dressed in blue gingham and
had a lace scarf tied under her chin, concealing her
hair completely. If it hadn't been for that brief turn of
the head I might not have recognized Colleen Bower.
Just in case she was bound somewhere else I went on
watching as she crossed the bridge over the dry creek
and entered the mission behind the others.

"I'll be damned," I said.

"What kind of odds you giving?" Junior asked.

Three Apaches mounted on slat-sided ponies trailed
me most of my first day at a distance of five hundred
yards, not even bothering to conceal themselves
when I turned in the saddle to look back. That meant
either they were just curious or had enough rein-
forcements nearby to make any action I might take a
topic of conversation that night while they were waiting for my brains to come to a boil. Since they knew
where I was anyway I built a fire after dark and
cooked my supper, but when I turned in I led the
claybank a hundred feet away from the embers and
spread my blanket there. In the morning they were
gone. Frightening the water out of lone white travelers is an Indian sport as old as Montezuma.

The streets of Socorro were crowded even for a
town that size of a Monday. I threaded my way between the buckboards and buggies and stepped down

in front of the livery, where Ole, the white-haired youth with the tired bones, was sitting on his bench in the shade of his flop brim.

"Give him oats and rub him down." I held out the reins.

He tipped his head back carefully, as if it might fall off its hinge, and screwed up his face against the sun. "I thought the sheriff run you out last week."

"I ran back. Oats. Rubdown." I jiggled the reins under his nose.

"Well, I ain't certain we got the room. Lots of folks in for the hanging. I'll tether him out here for a dollar, though. Feed's extra."

I chewed on it a second, then reached inside my pocket. His tongue bulged his cheek as he watched.

"Maybe two dollars," he said.

Without taking my hand out of my pocket I hooked the heel of my right boot under the edge of the bench and shoved. He showed me two soles in need of repair and went right on over in a creditable somersault. Lying on his stomach on a patch of ground past due for shoveling, he spat out gravel. "I'm going to the sheriff!"

"Save the leather, Ole. I'm on my way there now." I came up with a cartwheel and flipped it. It landed in front of his nose. "Rub him down good. I'll know if you give him anything but oats. Hay makes him windy. And I want him in a stall."

"We're full up!"

"Give him your room. He's not choosy."

The door to the county office was locked with a sign on it reading EXECUTION TODAY. I took the alley to the fenced-in courtyard behind the building. Jubilo

No-Last-Name, the full-time deputy, was standing inside the gate. He had his Creedmoor rifle and any joy his half-caste face might have held had died in the shade of his flat-brimmed Stetson.

"Where's your invitation?"

"I didn't take one, remember? I didn't think I'd be in town for it. I need to talk to the sheriff."

"He's a mite busy just now."

"I'll wait."

Nothing went on in his features. "Might as well wait inside as out."

"Without an invitation?"

"We're hanging a man today, mister. I don't see nothing to joke about."

"They're hanging someone somewhere every day," I said. "I don't see anything but."

He turned sideways to let me pass. It was a big yard, and popular as the condemned man might have been, Baronet could have spared himself worry about filling it. Even in a town as large and lively as Socorro, events worth attending and talking about after were separated by long quiet times during which many a frontiersman found leisure to wonder why he came west in the first place. Next to Shakespeare and a lewd woman an execution was the best excuse to avoid so much unwelcome self-knowledge. There was the usual ratio of three men to each woman, but plenty enough of the latter to warrant shaking the shelf creases out of the store suit and putting it on. In those days we duded up for hangings the same way we did for funerals and church, and in my trail clothes I was seriously underdressed for the occasion. Not that anyone paid me more than passing attention. That was reserved for the four men on the scaffold.

This was an impressive structure as such things went, it being low-bid business on the county budget and generally a good excuse for the builder to get rid of his warped and knotty lumber. The cornerposts were six-by-sixes, planed smooth as white siding, and appeared to have been set as many feet below ground as they stood above. There was a proper staircase of eight steps instead of a ladder, which as far as getting a man up it who doesn't want to go is no better than a rope, and the gallows itself was sixbraced to the platform and mortised at the yardarm. The whole thing looked as solid as a new barn.

Frank Baronet, in his black frock coat and gray pinch hat, shared the scaffold with a priest in full raiment including the swan's-neck headgear, a much less picturesque pudgy party with his shirt ballooning out under his vest whom I took for the hangman, and the guest of honor. Hernando Padilla would have made two of his Mexican barber counterpart in San Sábado, standing three inches taller than the sheriff and nearly twice as broad across the torso. He was in white shirtsleeves, striped pants, and stockings, with a leather harness strapped around his waist pinning his arms to his sides, and just before the hangman dropped the black hood over his head—standing on tiptoe to reach—I saw that his face was large and badly pockmarked, with the elaborately curled moustaches that are the signature of any tonsorial artist who takes pride in his profession. I wondered which he had used to dispatch Ernestine "Mexican Red"

Grosvenor, a razor or just his big hands with their long, oddly graceful fingers. I found out later he had split her skull with a cuspidor.

There being no final statements from the condemned, and the priest having finished reading from Ecclesiastes, the hangman snugged the big knot up under Padilla's left ear, paused with his hand on the lever, and tripped it. The bottom dropped out from under the man in the hood. His neck broke with a sharp report like a log snapping in a fireplace. He bounced twice, pumped his right leg several times as if trying to climb back up onto the platform, and swayed around in a half-circle. The audience let out its breath in a collective sigh and began shuffling toward the gate.

The priest was one of the last to go. Just as he passed me he broke wind, reached back to pluck his cassock out of the crease in his buttocks, and picked up his pace.

As Jubilo herded out the stragglers, Baronet and the hangman loosened the rope and lowered the dead man through the trap, under which two men with funeral coats on over clean overalls caught him and laid him in an unlined cedar box, grunting a little as they wedged in his shoulders. The sheriff shook the hangman's hand and glanced at me distractedly as he came down the steps. I fell in beside him and we entered the building through the back door. The cells were empty on both sides. He unlocked the door to the office, tossed his keys at the desk, hung up his hat, and began opening and closing drawers in the desk.

"How many of those you been to?" He found a bottle and a glass and stopped looking.

"A few."

"Ever get used to it?"

"I never thought I would until I was hanged my-self," I said. "It didn't take and now it's just like watching a branding."

"You won't require this then." He heeled the cork back into the bottle and emptied the glass down his throat. After putting both away he took the embroi-dered pillow off the swivel behind the desk, pounded it twice, and sat down, poking it behind his back and squirming around until he had contact where he wanted it. He looked up at me, blinking hard. "One of Whiteside's hands was at your place Friday night. He sat at my table yesterday. He said you had trouble."

"Marshal Ortiz is holding a prisoner for you at the mission. He'll never play any violins with his gun hand."

"I heard there was a man killed."

"You heard it all then. The third man got away." I watched his face, but that blink was distracting. It would serve him well at poker. "That's not the reason I'm here."

Jubilo came in the back way and I stopped talking. The sheriff told him to go eat. He looked at me with-out expression, then went out the front carrying his Creedmoor.

"Does he sleep with that rifle?" I asked.

"I wouldn't know. We haven't shared a bed." He waited.

I leaned back against the high counter and crossed my ankles. The big-bore Remington pistol was stick-ing out of the notch in his vest but I didn't think he could use either end of it in his present position without alerting me. "Before we talk you ought to know I just left Ole in front of the livery with his face in a pile of manure."

"How could you tell them apart?" He rocked back and forth on the swivel, stopped. "Give me the rest of it."

I gave him the rest of it, including the details Colleen and I had worked out the day after the shooting. He listened, blinking and lifting a hand on occasion to smooth one or the other of his handlebars.

"How much are we discussing?" he asked when I stopped.

"Two thousand. Less if we can get a good price on those fixtures Mrs. Bower mentioned."

"She is your best collateral. If she is as comely as they claim on the circuit, and maybe even if she is not, there isn't a cowboy or a miner in the territory who wouldn't lather up a good horse in order to say he played cards with Poker Annie. Or any female, comes to that. There is the little problem of a county ordinance against women gambling in public."

"Yours?"

"It was on the books when I came. Some fracas over a tinhorn from Kansas and his redheaded companion; I disremember the circumstances. I'm told that in Dodge City they get around a similar law by declaring the gaming room private and banning Chinamen from entering."

"We have no Chinamen in San Sábado."

"Then they should be easy to keep out. What are the terms?"

"Three percent per month and the note comes due at the end of a year."

"Ten percent is customary for me."

"No percent is customary for me. Three and a half percent."

"Half percentages require too much arithmetic. Eight."

"Five."

"Eight is as low as I go."

"Who supervises the collection at that rate?" I asked. "Your brother Ross?"

He had stopped blinking. "Ross is dead. He died in Mexico of wounds received in the fighting in Lincoln County."

"He handles a Springfield rifle well for a corpse."

He shifted in his seat suddenly and I placed my hand on the butt of the Deane-Adams. Crossing his legs, he smiled. "Five percent. I will send someone to collect the first of every month. Not my brother. You are mistaken about him."

"The papers will be ready for you to sign when you come to claim Abel Freestone. He is the man Marshal Ortiz is holding at the mission."

"Ortiz couldn't hold his dick in a high wind. Are you heading back today?"

"No, I am stopping at the Socorro and going back in the morning. I saw Apaches yesterday. If I have the choice I'll be rested and fresh when I see them next."

"They intended no mischief if you saw them. If you wait a few days Jubilo will go with you. I'm sending him for Freestone and he can bring back the loan papers. I cannot leave the county seat at tax time. He is an artist with that Creedmoor."

"I'll think about it. If you don't hear from me before he leaves I went back already."

I went from there to the railroad station to wire the details to Junior and Colleen. The operator, bald and green-faced under his eyeshade, squinted at my name. "You're Murdock? I was just about to relay this on to San Sábado." He tore a flimsy off his spike and held it out.

YOU LEFT YOUR WALKING STICK IN HELENA STOP YOU WILL FIND IT WAITING LARAMIE W T UNTIL THIRTY AUGUST TRACK THREE

It was unsigned. "When's the next train north?" I asked.

The operator called across to the clerk at the ticket window, who checked his board and called back. "Five fifteen."

"I need to add something to that telegram I gave you."

He handed it back. I thought, then added:

HAVE LINE ON PURCHASE PIANO LARAMIE BACK IN TEN DAYS

The operator looked up from counting. "I was in Laramie last month. I don't remember seeing a piano works."

I stared at him until he returned to his totaling.

The ride north was uneventful, meaning it was hot and sooty and about as smooth as sitting on a rockslide. Educational, too; when you sleep on your tailbone you discover parts of your body you never knew you had. At the station in Laramie I shaved in the gentleman's water closet beside two other bleary-eyed travelers along life's highway. We couldn't have shed much more blood if we'd started a razor fight.

A porter directed me to Track 3, a siding with grass growing between the rails, occupied solely by a redwood Pullman with curtains in the windows. I mounted the platform, rapped on the door, received an invitation, checked my boots for mud, and entered. The inside was all paneling and red plush and crockery lamps with milky glass shades, in the midst of which its only inhabitant, seated in a big yellow leather wingback chair with studs, looked like a plain stone in a baroque setting.

"Well, Deputy, you are almost late," announced Judge Blackthorne. "I hope this saloonkeeping episode hasn't made you forget whom you're working for."

## ⌇ 9 ⌇

HARLAN A. BLACKTHORNE had once been described by a
member of the party to which he ostensibly belonged
as a "vest-pocket Lincoln." The statement was not intended as a compliment. Built along Honest Abe's
narrow lines, with chin whiskers, a high arid brow
capped with a swirl of blue-black hair, and prominent
bones, he would have required something more lofty
than his bankers' heels to deal with the Great Eman-
cipator on any level other than face-to-cravat. A
forty-year-old error in his military record reckoned
his height at five feet six and he was vain enough to
cite it still, but I knew for a certainty that the army
had been uncharacteristically generous by at least
three inches. The toes of his custom boots barely
touched the floor while he was planted in the big
chair.

His smile, which was a fixed thing with no amuse-
ment in it and a source of consternation for his politi-

cal enemies and the defendants who appeared before him, was more reminiscent of President Washington's in the portrait that hung in his courtroom. It concealed his total want of teeth. I'd never known him to wear his temporaries at any time except when he was trying a case. I had long since left off asking myself why a man who spent so much time and personal assets on his tailoring—today it was a gray Norfolk and matching trousers with his lucky gold horseshoe tacked to a purple ascot—never took the trouble to visit a dentist who knew his trade. But then I will go to Glory not knowing the man, though I spent the better part of my middle years earning his good opinion.

"I wouldn't make light of this saloonkeeping business, sir," I said, looking for a place to lay my hat. "The hours are better than federal work and I don't have to pay to bury the men I shoot."

"You've shot someone so soon? If I thought your intention was to improve upon your previous time I never would have agreed to let you go."

I gave up looking and sat down in a padded rocker, crossing my legs and hanging the hat on my knee. "They don't call me Satan's Sixgun for sport."

"Yes, it seems all of Helena is reading the man Hookstratton's gentle prose. I expect to see it entered into the Congressional Record any day. Those carpetbaggers in Washington will stop at nothing to cause me grief." He rapped a finger on the arm of his chair for lack of a gavel. "I am sorry I had to bring you all this way, Deputy. Rail travel is a trial in this climate."

"More so for some of us than for others."

"I have temporary use of the salon car, no more.

I am fortunate in my acquaintances. The apology stands."

"It's unnecessary. You can't know what a relief it is to be someplace where Billy the Kid didn't shoot anyone."

"Who?"

"Nobody important, sir. We have to discuss this walking stick device. I doubt there is anyone in Montana who hasn't seen through it by now."

"I did not employ it to deceive anyone in Montana. So far as the territory of New Mexico is concerned, Blackthorne is a name from your past. In any case it brought you here."

"The question is, what brought you? Your honor."

"We shall come to that presently. What have you to report?"

"I'm in partnership with Junior Harper as planned. He thinks I took him up on his offer because I'm weary of keeping the peace. It might surprise you to learn how little convincing that required."

"You are impertinent. Proceed."

"Something we didn't plan on is named Colleen Bower. Junior cut her in for a full third before I arrived."

"The name is not unfamiliar."

"She's known more widely on the circuit as Poker Annie. I had dealings with her two years ago in Breen."

"Ah." His *Ah* had more sides than a roundhouse. How much he knew or speculated beyond what I had told him of the happenings in Breen was anyone's guess.

"She has San Francisco ideas for the Apache Princess. All of them involve money. I suggested we borrow it from Frank Baronet."

"Elephantine."

"You haven't met him, sir. Anything less is lost on him. Mrs. Bower agreed to the proposition, although Junior did not. It was a majority decision and I took it to Baronet. He went for it like a steer for water. He is all cash-and-carry."

"Anything else?"

I told him about the pistol-whipping I had received in Socorro City and the man the sheriff killed who claimed to have seen Ross Baronet alive in Mexico. The Judge smoothed his whiskers, always a sign he was troubled.

"A dead man who happened to say something in your presence and a battery on your person which you confess to have invited through your own intemperance; is that the extent of your grounds?"

"Yes. Well, except for Ross Baronet attempting to rob the Princess Friday night."

*"Thunderation!"*

I had seldom heard him bellow, and then only at certain attorneys from back East who thought the law they had learned from their professors assayed out higher than the grade he had panned behind his rude bench. It made the glass in the car ring. He gripped the arms of the chair hard until the spasm passed.

"Again I apologize," he said in his customary judicial tone. "You are in San Sábado as a favor to me and I have no right to dictate the manner in which you impart information. I do request that you refrain from the dramatic."

"I'm sorry, sir." I gave him the full account, ending with Dutch Tim's burial. As he listened he crossed his legs, something he did when particularly pleased, an event more rare for him than shouting.

"A distinct touch, that headboard. Tweaking Ross Baronet over the loss of his man should help to draw suspicion from your eagerness to enter into a transaction with his brother." He put the leg down. "My purpose in arranging this meeting is to inform you that we must move up our schedule."

"I wasn't aware we had one."

He went on as if I hadn't spoken. "It has come to my attention that certain Democrats in the Congress are conspiring to propose amnesty for all those currently wanted for crimes committed during the war in Lincoln County. The measure will be introduced in the Senate next month in time to pass through both houses before the November elections. Given his preference the American voter will see a scoundrel set free. It is that old revolutionary curse."

"Do you think the president will sign such a bill?"

"Who is to say who will be president when it reaches the White House? Garfield does not appear to be recovering from that assassin's bullet he took last month. Chester Arthur is a Hudson River hack who blows with Tammany, and that Irish crowd will side with Dolan. If we do not move swiftly we may be forced not only to release our covey, but to present them with the net as well in fee simple for the inconvenience."

He paused a beat in case I cared to jump in. I didn't, and he sat back as far as he ever did, perhaps an inch.

"Grapeshot tore open my belly at the siege of Monterrey," he said. "My intestines were lying on the ground beside me. A medical officer commanded an orderly to let me die and go help some other wretch who could still be saved. Sergeant Uriah Spooner leveled his musket at the officer and informed the orderly that if I were not removed to the field station immediately the American expeditionary force in Mexico would be shy one brass-buttons. For this offense he was arrested, court-martialed, and sentenced to death. I was too ill to testify at the first hearing, but when another was convened to review the evidence I appeared on a stretcher. I dislike quoting myself. Suffice it to say I found my calling that day and I have cleaved to the law ever since. Spooner's sentence was commuted to five years' penal servitude and a dishonorable discharge.

"I was present at his wedding ceremony and again at the christening of his only son. I missed his funeral two years ago as I was hearing a capital case at the time. When I learned that Ross Baronet and whoever was with him had killed young Dave Spooner and his wife in Lincoln County, the scars of that old injury began to sting for the first time in thirty-five years. They are stinging yet. I can only conclude that they will continue to vex me until justice is served."

He tapped the arm of his chair. Tension fled from the car like heat through a shattered window. "One man's sore stomach is scarcely grounds for federal action. My jurisdiction does not cover crimes committed in New Mexico. I therefore accepted your badge and papers and wished you Godspeed on your sojourn into private enterprise. The fact that the enterprise should be located in the county where Frank Baronet presides was mere coincidence."

"Helped along by a good memory," I said. "Dave and Vespa Spooner were still nursing cattle and enjoying good health at the time Junior approached me. I always did take a while deciding my future."

We were coming perilously close to an expression of gratitude, but he side-railed it as only a civil servant can who has managed to survive three presidential administrations and an impeachment attempt. "I want the men responsible for these murders arrested, tried, and convicted before the politicians can act. Since the territory was under martial law at the time of the atrocity I want the case heard in federal court where the Dolan influence is less profound. I do not insist that it be my court, but neither will I shirk my responsibilities should the venue shift to Montana to avoid local prejudice. I fear that the delay of even a month may be fatal."

I uncrossed my legs and circled my hatbrim through my fingers. "Well, we can arrest Ross for the attempted robbery of the saloon. We can try to peg Dutch Tim's death on him. It's a stretch, but if we play him smart he might be persuaded to talk about the raid on the Spooner ranch in return for the promise of a sentence lighter than death."

"If he pulled the trigger he will hang."

"He won't talk then. You can bend a rifle barrel over the skulls of these southwestern road agents for twice your month and they will just laugh at you. They all fear the rope, but if it's swing for Dutch Tim or swing for the Spooners I don't see the choice in it. Nor will he."

He touched his beard. "Life then. But only if he gives up his companions and the name of the man who planned the raid."

"That would be Frank or I miss my guess. There is the little problem of tracking Ross down. The trail is cold. I had hopes of getting to him by way of Frank's wallet but that will require more time than we have. Also if I take out after him alone it will look wrong. I'm not a lawman down there, remember. As a saloonkeeper I'm only out the price of a burial. The holdup didn't go through."

"Who keeps the peace in San Sábado?"

"No one. A fat Mexican named Ortiz pins himself to the town star when he is not weeding his roses or shouting at his many children."

"Ortiz? Intriguing. We captured a young lieutenant by that name at Cerro Gordo. On the second night he strangled one of the sentries guarding him and shot another with the man's musket. He bayoneted a third on his way over the stockade. The following day he was observed fighting alongside his countrymen. I haven't thought of him in years."

"It isn't the same Ortiz."

"Likely not. The surname is a common one. You must try to bring this man around. Fewer questions will be asked if you assist him in Ross Baronet's arrest."

"It will be like assisting a boulder up Granite Peak. One question, sir."

He read the face of a mantel clock mollusked over with gilt cupids. "Make it brief. You have just time to board the Santa Fe southbound. It leaves at one forty-five."

"Pinholster is the deputy with all the experience under cover. He was a Wells Fargo agent for four years. Arnsen knows that Socorro country like the clay under his nails and O'Donnell has been with you longer than anyone and has more of your trust than all the rest of us put together. Why did you ask me to help in this?"

"I do not submit my decisions to committee, Deputy. You will miss your train."

"That's too thin, sir. It works when we are judge and officer of the court, but you said it yourself, this is a personal favor. The question deserves an answer."

"You may be right. I may even concur. That does not mean I will provide it."

I rose. "It doesn't signify anyway because I've guessed it. Pinholster and O'Donnell are as straight as a short drop. They bring their men in alive. So does Arnsen, but for a different reason. He's close with his purse and would avoid paying a federal burying fee at the cost of his own skin. I make the effort, but it doesn't always answer and I will kill a man without thought if he brings me grief. That's why you chose me, not because I'm loyal or dependable. The odds are better than even I will spare the United States the bother of a trial, which might delay things long enough for Dolan to get back from Washington City with his box of pardons. This way he will be forced to nail them up in matching coffins."

"You are misled."

"I've never thought so."

"Good hunting, Deputy. Wire me in Helena when you have something worth sharing."

I left him then surrounded by his borrowed bric-abrac. You can read about Judge Harlan Amsdill Black-thorne in the florid memoirs of the tenderheel attor-neys who pleaded in his courtroom, about his Old Testament views and the forty-six men and one woman he sentenced to hang in their observance, and it's all true. But something he said on the subject of justice while handing down one of those sentences is carved over a doorway at the Harvard School of Law, and the memoirs are all mustering dust and dead flies on some forgotten shelf. The fact that I don't understand those chiseled words any more than I did the man who spoke them is neither here nor there. He had more enemies than Custer on his hill but few peers.

# 10

THE SAME THREE Apaches, or three from the same litter if not them, locked on to my trail half a day out of Socorro City on the way home, and inside two hours had closed to within a thousand feet. That was close enough to show their long shirts sashed about the waist and their hide leggings, proof against mescal spines and diamondbacks, and too close for me. Two had lances. The third carried a carbine behind his shoulder and what looked like extra cartridge belts slung from the horn of a proper saddle. Sensing them, the claybank told me in a hundred little ways what it thought of the situation, but I held it to a brisk walk, conserving vinegar for when a dash might be required. It seemed to understand and made only a token try at throwing the bit.

Another good reason not to run was I was in no hurry to quit that rolling foothill country west of the

Oscuros until nightfall, when I might have a chance to cross the Jornada del Muerto under cover of darkness, which was the only cover that flat desert land offered. That was the plan, and the only thing wrong with it was it depended largely on Indian patience, a commodity rarer there than springwater.

It ran out in another hour. Something struck the parched earth in front of us and to the left with a *tuck* sound and a ball of dust. The report reached me a beat behind, bent in the middle and dulled by distance, *palop*, a pebble dropping into a shallow pool. I didn't look around, but quirted the reins across the gelding's withers and leaned over the pommel, offering less opposition to the wind while reducing the target. The bottom dropped out of the horse's gait. Its long legs chewed up ground and the wind pasted the front of my hatbrim to the crown. I thanked John Whiteside and myself for our taste in mounts. A big rump has all the mechanics necessary to push an animal along.

There may have been other shots. Probably there were. I didn't listen. I was too busy looking for a place to come to ground. You can't outrun Indians, there is no use trying. Apaches especially will overtake you on a bag of buffalo grass and bones no matter if you are riding von Bismarck's finest. They run them on pure mean, of which they have an unlimited supply.

The outlook held small promise. The foothills themselves lay too far to the east and there was nothing handy in the way of a breastwork. I risked a look back and saw all three riders closing, the one with the carbine foremost. He would be coming hardest to give himself time to draw rein and make a stationary shot

before I fell out of range. Savages were poor marks-
men as a rule and disliked wasting lead on a moving
target from a moving platform.

Well, hell. Three hundred dollars doesn't go as far
as it used to.

I reached back and unsheathed the curve-bladed
skinning knife I'd carried since my winter wolfing
days up on the Cut Bank. Shooting horses is prefera-
ble to cutting their throats for a variety of reasons, but
not when you are in for a long siege and can't spare
the ammunition. Next to a clay hill a supine carcass is
the best thing in nature for stopping enemy fire.

I was just about to dig in, leap off, and cut when I
spotted something sweet to the southwest. This was a
long gentle swell of land much like all the others in
that region but with the attraction of a line of junipers
behind which a man could crouch and give battle
without making a bull's-eye of himself into the bar-
gain. I veered that way and raked the claybank's
flanks, drawing blood and a squeal of pain and rage
and a burst of speed that almost snatched my hat off
my head. A spark flew off a flat rock just to my right,
a snap shot intended to steer me away from the junipers. I hoped the nearness was a fluke. Trust me to
draw the only sharpshooter in moccasins this side of
Buffalo Bill's Wild West.

Going around the end of the juniper bank was the
long route. I headed straight for it. I hoped the gelding
was game and not one of those treasures that set their
brakes at the prospect of leaving the earth for any reason. In the end it wouldn't matter, though, because
either way I was going over, and if I made the trip
alone and landed on my head and broke my neck I'd

make a poor subject for the Apache notion of entertainment. I clawed for meat once again. I could tell by the answering shudder that I had made a friend for life. It's just as well they don't have trigger fingers.

And then we were airborne, the drumming gone from below and only the wind whistling past my ears to take my thoughts off what was behind and what might be ahead. The claybank grunted when it pushed off. Only the whites of its eyes showed on the way aloft. A branch brushed my leg and then we were clear. Open ground swept away in front of us. My teeth snapped together when we struck down, a pair of disks scraped against each other in my lower back. I gave the horse a few yards to find its footing and then I leaned back on the reins, turning its head and slipping my left foot out of the stirrup. When it went down I leaped clear, landed on both feet, and snapped the Winchester out of its scabbard. By the time the claybank got up and shook itself I was down on my stomach and drawing a bead between junipers.

The three braves had slowed their approach, reading my mind. At that distance I couldn't tell if they were painted, but then I'd gotten drunk in Helena one night with a former aide of General George Crook's who told me Apaches wore theirs on the inside where it never rubbed off. Resting my forearms on the slight rise, I laid the front sight on the arch of the rib cage of the one with the carbine, took a breath, let out half of it, and squeezed the trigger. A rooster tail of dust bristled in front of his mount's left forefoot.

Damn the duplicity of that sand country. The heat made a long lens of the air near the ground and made everything look closer than it was. All three Indians hauled back on their hair bridles and retreated farther out of range.

While they parleyed I crawled back toward the claybank for my canteen and the extra cartridge boxes in my saddle wallets. The damn beast was still indignant over having been made to soil its coat and shied, but I lunged for a dragging rein and hauled it close hand over hand. When I had what I needed I crawled back to my rise. One of the Apaches was missing along with his horse.

How they manage to move around in open prairie and stay invisible is one for those eggheads in Chicago who take them apart like frogs and study the pieces and publish papers on the subject. It didn't much matter, because I knew where he was going. I measured the height of the sun with my hands and decided there would still be enough light for him to see what he was doing by the time he got behind me. At least I still had a view of the one with the firepower.

Not that dying from a lance thrust instead of a bullet makes much difference beyond what they carve on the headstone.

Desert heat doesn't follow any of the standard rules. You'd expect it to be worst when the sun is straight up, but a hat will protect you from it then. When the only shade for miles is on the wrong side of the shrubbery you're using for cover, there is no hiding from that afternoon slant. I turned up my collar and unfastened my cuffs and pulled them down over the backs of my hands, but I could feel my skin turning red and shrinking under the fabric. Pinheads of sweat marched along the edge of my leather hatband and tracked down into my eyes, stinging like fire ants. The water in the canteen tasted like hot metal. I wanted the Montana snow, blue as the veins in Colleen Bower's throat with the mountain runoff coursing black through it carrying shards of white ice. All this time the two Indians sat their ponies, as motionless as buttes and just as easy to reason with. I was just something to break up the day, that and a horse and a long and a short gun to bring the two braves with lances into the nineteenth century.

I thumbed a fresh cartridge into the magazine to replace the one I'd fired and took another shot at the man with the carbine. There was no reason for it other than to spook his horse and spoil his mood. For all the reaction the pinto showed I might as well have waved my hat and sung Dixie. I guessed I was becoming addled by the heat and worry.

A rifle cracked. I swore it was behind me, but that country was full of distortions and I wasn't thinking right to begin with. I did know that the Indian with the carbine hadn't moved and there was no smoke in his direction. I rolled over, reversed ends, and squinted through the ground haze to the west at a rider coming hard my way. I swept a sleeve across my eyes to clear away the sweat, polished them with the heels of my hands, but he was still there, and closer. His horse's hoofbeats reached me then, hollowed out by distance and warped by heatwaves. I worked the Winchester's lever and settled the iron sight in the middle of the shimmering bulk. Either the man they'd sent to shut the back door had a long gun I didn't know about or a fourth had joined the fracas. I fired. I will still testify that I saw the bullet leave the barrel and find its mark. Fear and sunstroke are like peyote. You will see things.

What counted was my target heeled over and struck the ground with a grunt that was real enough. After a couple of seconds it separated into two pieces, one smaller than the other, and when the smaller piece rose from a crawl to a crouch I knew I'd deprived the rider of his horse. I racked in another shell and took aim on the man.

"Mother of God, don't shoot *me*!"

I knew there were Christian Indians and had met one or two, but rarely enough to make me hesitate with my finger on the trigger this time. That was sufficient time to see that this was no Apache. He ran like a white man for one thing, long strides with his toes pointed out, and his high boots and striped trousers and white shirt were store-bought. In another second I recognized the flat-brimmed Stetson and the rifle he carried, ready to raise against me if I failed to lower the Winchester.

"Jubilo, is that you?"

"Murdock?"

I said it was. The deputy sheriff of Socorro sprinted the rest of the distance and dived headfirst into the shallow depression, holding up the Creedmoor to keep sand out of the action. He crawled forward to face me. "I just shot a damn Apache off a horse for you. If I knew you was fixing to shoot *my* horse I'd of caught his."

"Next time raise a yell. I didn't know you from Geronimo."

"See if I come help a white man out of a hole next

time." The expression on his half-caste face was un-readable. "Did you even know you had a red bastard climbing your back fence?"

"Knew it. Couldn't fix it. Care to see what's up front?" Without waiting for an answer I rolled over and slithered back up to the shrub line. He joined me a second later.

"Shit, I'd of thought Satan's Sixgun was more than a fight for two little *mimbreños.*"

"Three. And I didn't write that book."

"They'll be getting restless in a minute. They're thinking their pard should be on you by now."

"Maybe they'll come in range to investigate."

"Why wait?" He rolled back the Creedmoor's Remington block, removed the long cartridge, blew inside, and replaced the cartridge. He rolled the block forward.

"You any good with that competition rifle?" I asked.

"I was Lincoln County champion two years in a row. One thing they like to do in Lincoln is shoot." He unfolded the sight, locked it into placc, looked through it at the waiting Apaches, adjusted the slide, looked through it again, and stretched out full length, finding a comfortable spot to rest his cheek. The Indi-ans were straining their necks to see past the junipers. They didn't appear agitated. They knew they were well outside the Winchester's reach.

Jubilo pressed the trigger. The gun roared, backing up against his shoulder. Far away across the plain the Apache with the carbine, still craning for a good look, threw back his arms and slid over sideways. While he was still falling Jubilo opened the block, plucked out the hot shell, poked in a fresh cartridge, slammed home the action, and took aim again. But the other Apache was already moving, wheeling his horse and slapping its rump. Jubilo fired again.

"Miss."

"Maybe." He extracted the casing and reloaded. "The sons of bitches are like antelope and will run forty miles with the top of their heart blowed to hell."

But he didn't fire the third cartridge. The Indian now was out of range of even the big rolling-block and moving fast. Jubilo glanced at the sun. "We'll wait here till dark. No telling how close his other friends are and this is the only cover for miles. Such as it is."

The Apache he'd shot wasn't moving. His horse had bolted when he fell. I calculated the distance at right around four hundred yards.

"The sheriff said you were an artist," I said.

"I am when it comes to drawing a bead." He sat up and brushed sand off his cheek. "What you doing way out here? I thought you went back to San Sábado a week ago."

"I had business up north. What are you?"

"Sheriff sent me your way to pick up a prisoner. I'm just on my way back."

"Where's the prisoner?" I had almost forgotten about Abel Freestone.

"Dead as Andy Jackson. When that hand swoll up and turned black he wouldn't let the sawbones take it off and he was gone the next day."

"Hard luck."

"Not so bad. I had to bring back some papers anyway."

I watched him wiping dust off the Creedmoor with his bandanna. He had slender hands for a Mexican and appeared to be fussy about the nails. That was an old story among gun men. It started with taking care of your weapon, spread to your hands, and before you knew it you were wearing red velvet coats and perfume in your hair like Hickok. "How long have you been working with Frank Baronet?"

"Just since last fall as deputy. I come back up from Mexico after he got elected."

"I mean since before that."

"Two years. I knew his brother Ross and we all hired on to regulate for the Dolan-Murphy combine. We had us some times, Frank and Ross and me, till that carpetbagger Wallace took over and brung in the army. There was a stir over this cow thief that got killed, him and his whore wife, and Ross and me went down to Chihuahua. He had a ball in his hip and died of mortification there."

"Were you with him then?"

"No, we split up and I only heard about it when I come back here. I scouted some before Lincoln County. Before that I worked for Juárez."

"You fought in the revolution?"

"The last part. I was just a yonker. This old one-eyed colonel stuck a Jaeger needle gun in my hands and showed me which end to point and which end to pull on and before I knew it I was knocking down *federales* like apples. Turned out I had a gift for it. Then the war went and ended."

"What does a sharpshooter do in peacetime?"

"You'd never guess. Growing up on the border I had as much English as I had Spanish, so they gave me a job collecting taxes in El Paso del Norte." He shook his head. "Gawd Almighty, don't them butchers and barbers hate to pay their share. I shot one by accident and that's when I decided to come north the first time. The revolution had went to hell anyway by then. Juárez didn't turn out to be no better than what we had before."

"That why you threw in with the Baronets?"

"You're just down on Frank on account of he buffaloed you that time. That weren't nothing. If he didn't like you they'd of scooped up your brains with the horseshit."

"That's no answer."

"I guess not. Someone told me they got this fancy notion back East about always mounting a horse from the left. I figure they don't ride much. Out here it don't matter which side you climb up on. They're both of them just as bad." He watched me peering between bushes. "Don't expect him back. Moving at night's just smart in case there are other parties out haring around. They ain't cowards, mind. That ain't the reason he lit out. Those lazy sons of bitches get ants when something starts to look like work. I'm Comanche on my father's side and I guess I know them."

"I'm glad you happened along. Dealing with them alone might have cost me another day."

"Not to mention your hair and both ears. Apaches are partial to ears. They string them around their necks so they can listen to the other side."

I reloaded the Winchester's magazine. "I heard the same thing about the Sioux. Also the Nez Percé and the Cheyenne and the Blackfoot. I've fought them all and a few others whose names I can't pronounce and I never saw an ear necklace on one of them."

"Well, if it ain't true it ought to be. You can make a case for them tribes you mentioned defending their land and all. Patch got nothing to defend. Nobody wants this here desert country but him. There's nothing meaner than an Apache brave, unless it's an Apache squaw. Neither one will eat snake. They say it's because of their religion. I say it's professional courtesy."

"I'm starting to understand. You don't like them."

"The other tribes don't like them any better than me. That's why they drove them out of every place worth living in."

"Going just by that," I said, "you're just as wicked as they are."

He smiled for only the second time since we'd met. "Well, hell's bells. I never said I wasn't."

That was the end of conversation. We settled in to wait for darkness. I didn't want any more talk in any case. I was on the edge of liking him, and it would just get in the way when the time came to kill him.

## ᵞ⌐ᴏ 11 ᴏᴄᴌ

WHICHEVER GOD LOOKS after snipers and saloonkeepers was on duty that night, and we stole away under a rustlers' moon bright enough to show prairie dog holes but not us. Jubilo's horse, a blaze-face roan fifteen years old, was cold when we stopped to strip it of as much gear as we could carry. The claybank didn't encourage being loaded down with two full-grown men and their necessaries, but it seemed to sense how close it had come to sharing the roan's fate and didn't become obnoxious. We entered San Sábado at first light, iron shoes chiming against the empty hardpack street. In front of the livery we stepped down and I kicked the door until the Yaquí came out to take the reins. He wasn't long coming and was fully dressed. I don't know when he slept.

He led the claybank to a stall and brought out a bay mare for Jubilo's inspection. The deputy checked its teeth and fetlocks and looked in its ears.

"Hundred," he said.

"*Doscientos*," said the Indian.

"It's too early to dicker. Hundred and twenty-five."

"*Doscientos*," said the Indian.

"She's twelve if she's a day. If she was a woman I wouldn't pay more than fifty cents for all night."

"*Doscientos*," said the Indian.

Jubilo looked at me. "That the only Spanish he knows?"

"You're the Indian expert."

"Hundred and fifty. Now, that's the limit."

"*Doscientos*," said the Indian.

"Shit. I'll give you a county marker."

The Indian shook his head. "Cash money."

He said shit again, unbuttoned his shirt, and unwrapped a money belt from around his waist. Thick white scars curled around his brown hairless torso from behind in a pattern familiar to me. I wondered whose lash it had been, Maximilian's or Juárez's.

He gave the Yaquí another dollar to feed and rub down the bay and we walked out carrying our gear. "You can bunk in my room," I said. "I guess I owe you a roof."

"I'll spread my roll uptrail."

"I'm told I don't snore."

"It ain't that, it's the being shut in. I got me a little room off the cells in Socorro but I don't use it much."

We divided without a word in front of the Apache Princess. I didn't know if we'd see each other again except through our sights.

I caught two hours' sleep and was shaving over the basin in the room when the door opened from the outside stairs. Ford Harper's only son grinned at me sloppily past the barrel of the Deane-Adams. He had on his sheepskin over the paisley vest and was carrying a bundle under one arm. "Put it up, son," he said. "I didn't steal that much while you were gone."

I returned the revolver to the belt hanging from the bedpost. "You've been around these townies too long, Junior. In the old days it was knock or get shot."

"Knock on what? I've went through more doors to see you in the past month than I did all the time we punched cows. How was Laramie?"

"Same as Virginia City, only smaller and farther north." I scraped my throat.

"Where's the piano?"

I hesitated. I'd almost forgotten the wire I'd sent from Socorro City. "They wanted too much."

"That's a long way to go to come back empty-handed."

"Well, once you're on the road." I changed the subject. "I see you're not in the same condition. What's in the bundle?"

He threw it on the bed. "You tell me. It came for you Friday on the Butterfield. Not knowing what's in it I didn't think it was safe to leave it in your room unattended." He slumped into the room's only chair, a Morris with faded tapestry cushions. "I hear you rode in double this morning with Baronet's deputy. Run into trouble?"

"He killed two Apaches. I killed his horse and we quit even."

"Is he as good with that rifle as they claim?"

"He is if they claim he hits what he aims at." I

wiped off the remaining lather and reached for my shirt. "I hear Abel Freestone didn't make it."

"The padre wasn't happy. The ventilation is poor at the mission and there is not enough quicklime in the territory to kill the smell of putrification coming up from below during High Mass. He has asked Ortiz to find another place to store his prisoners."

"Has anyone heard anything of Ross Baronet?"

"Someone stuck up a pack train outside Las Cruces Sunday and got off with six thousand in silver. They left eight Mexicans dead and the mules aren't talking. My better judgment says it was not Jesse James."

"Eight dead. That's raw even for a Baronet."

"Did I mention they were Mexicans?"

"Still it's taking a chance. Frank cannot have approved of it."

"Possibly not. Two of those killed were vaqueros hiring out before the fall drive. Talk is President Díaz will wire an official protest to Washington City by way of Governor Wallace. The vaqueros belonged to Don Segundo and guess who bankrolled the Díaz revolution?"

"No wonder Frank insists Ross is dead," I said. "It's a fond wish."

"The business will come to nothing. Garfield is busy bleeding into a pan and Wallace can't move without federal help. Meanwhile Ross is no concern for us. By now he's in a cave in Chihuahua counting his booty."

I sat down on the bed with my back to him and

pulled on my boots. He was a good poker reader and might see the disappointment on my face.

"What's Colleen about?" I asked. "Shot anyone lately?"

"She's out riding with Eille MacNutt."

I turned to look at him. His treadle jaw was set.

"It started the day you left for Socorro City. She has the notion we can come to some sort of business arrangement with the Mare's Nest. You will have to get it from her. Every time she explains it to me I get a headache." He forked out a nickel-plated watch I recognized as his father's. "They should be getting back about now. No buggy horse will tolerate hauling around a man of MacNutt's size much past an hour."

"I thought the whole idea of this investment was you wanted to run a saloon. It seems to me all you've been doing is watching someone else run it."

"I admit I'm not the man you are, Page. I can't manage a business and Poker Annie too."

I stood and put on my hat.

"Ain't you going to open your package?" he asked.

"Later. I know what's in it." I went out.

The Mare's Nest conducted business in an adobe pile that probably dated back to San Sábado's founding and showed every repair job that had ever been done on it in a hundred mottled patches like a topographical map. Its name was painted directly on its surface in large inexpert capitals without an apostrophe. At the moment an obese yellow cat was the only thing inhabiting the front porch, curled up in a splayed rocker wired together at the weak points. Thus far in my tenure I had never seen anyone else in the chair except Eille MacNutt. He was there when I came out in the morning and he was there when I climbed the Princess's outside stairs to bed, and he never seemed to feel the urge to rock, really an inhuman feat when you thought about it. He couldn't have weighed less than three hundred and might have gone four; I had yet to see him standing and so didn't have a height to figure in. I was certain he'd taken on most of those pounds since coming to town, because I couldn't picture him in his present state sitting on a wagon seat, much less a saddle. The very thought of him riding in a buggy, with or without female companionship, brought forth visions of a glacier on a velocipede.

"Don't be shy, long-tall. There's lots more to see inside."

The woman slouching in the doorway of the building wasn't the prettiest in a string not known for its beauty. Clad in an undyed muslin shift with enough sunlight coming in the back windows to show she wore nothing underneath, she was gaunt with bad skin and worse teeth that she covered with one hand when she talked. The paint she wore might have been applied by whoever had done the sign on the building, emphasizing all her worst features, and her brown hair was cropped suspiciously short, as if to discourage lice. She went by Clara California. I doubted she came from there. San Sábado was the kind of place you left behind on your way to California. She looked forty and was probably twenty-five. It was cruel work for the pay.

"That's a lie," I said. "I've seen inside. And I'm not tall."

"You're all of you the same height laying down."
There was Texas in her speech, or more likely the Nations. She had Cherokee bones. "Everyone else is
asleep. You can have the morning rate."

"Thanks. I'm waiting for someone."

"Not that Adabelle. She's all shine and no heat.
It'll freeze and fall off."

"Someone else."

"Too bad, long-tall. Too bad." She withdrew inside.

In a little while a green phaeton with ivory trim
rattled up the street behind a gray and a black with
blinders and stopped in front of the building. Actually
it didn't do much rattling. The ballast provided by the
man in the driver's seat pasted the wheels to the
hardpack as solidly as a load of iron stoves. Eille Mac-
Nutt was a tailoring challenge in several yards of
crinkly seersucker and a straw skimmer with a red
silk band, tilted rakishly over one eye. His features
were crowded around a toothbrush moustache in the
exact center of his big face like too little furniture in a
huge room and when he winched himself up, using
both hands and leaning the carriage far over on its
springs, a thick cloud of lavender flooded my nostrils.
I didn't fault him for it. Fat men suffered in that desert
heat and he had done what he could about the inevitable acrid odor with the help of the toiletry section in
the Montgomery Ward catalogue.

He got down to the street without help and
reached up a hand to his passenger. Colleen Bower
laid her gloved one in it, lifted her hem, and stepped
down. She wore an embroidered wrap to protect her
blue dress from dust and a wedge-shaped hat planted

with flowers and secured by a plain white scarf tied under her chin.

"Thank you so much, Mr. MacNutt. You're a wizard with horses."

"I claim no credit. Your charming presence is more effective than any quirt." His voice was callow. The weight made him look older, but he was probably still in his twenties. He saw me and nodded. "Murdock."

"MacNutt." It was as much conversation as had passed between us since we'd met.

"Good morning, Page. I hope your trip was pleasant." Colleen raised a hand to let me help her up onto the boardwalk.

I kept both of mine in my pockets. "I still have my hair. That's pleasant for New Mexico."

MacNutt mounted the walk and performed the gentlemanly duty. "There's no need to end this just because the animals are tired," he told her. "I have a bottle of Napoleon in my office."

"Another time, perhaps. Thank you for an enchanting drive." She took my arm and inserted pressure on the bicep. We started walking in the direction of the Apache Princess.

"It's at least a hundred yards to the door," I said. "Shall I hitch up the buckboard?"

A muscle worked in her jaw. "The first time I heard your name I thought it sounded chivalric. I had much to learn."

"Is that what it took to get you to go riding with the Great Divide?"

"A trim waist is hardly a substitute for good manners."

"If you're that smitten I'm surprised you didn't take him up on the brandy."

"Do you want to hear the proposition I put to him or not?"

"Does it matter what your partners want?"

"It helps when they are here to consult."

"I am here."

"So you are. It occurred to me while you were gone that we are not in competition with the Mare's Nest at all. Our customers come to drink and play cards. They can do that at MacNutt's as well, but it is not their primary concern."

"Yes, Clara California gave me that impression."

"Oh?"

"I interrupted you."

"So you did. I proposed to MacNutt that since we are not in the same business we could help each other by issuing vouchers. If they visit the Nest first and spend money they will receive a certificate to be redeemed for chips or a drink at the Princess. If they visit the Princess first and spend money we will issue them a token to be applied against the price of companionship at the Nest. As things stand, fully half our respective clientele winds up spending the entire evening at one establishment or the other. This way they will patronize both."

"At a discount."

"Just for one turn of the cards or one drink. If they stopped there we would have been out of business before this."

"It's not the same with companionship," I said.

"That's the beauty of the arrangement. MacNutt's

head runs toward figures, not the nature of man. Most of the advantage is ours."

"Sooner or later he is bound to see that."

"By then there will be customers enough to go around. Meanwhile we will have more capital to invest in the improvements we discussed."

"And until then you intend to buy time by going riding with Eille MacNutt."

We were in front of the saloon. She stopped walking and intercepted my gaze. "Yes."

"What happens when he finds out what you've been doing?"

"I grew up on the circuit," she said. "I would not have done so had I not learned how to take care of myself."

"That purse pistol won't get you out of everything."

"It has so far."

"Is this what you were up to when they ran you out of El Paso?"

"That was a misunderstanding."

"Did it have to do with that band you're wearing?"

She touched it involuntarily; smiled, but not with her eyes. "For someone who no longer keeps the peace you are asking a lot of questions."

"You're forgetting our silent partner. Frank Baronet is already worried about his brother's banditry and what it may mean for his position as sheriff. A falling-out involving an enterprise he's connected with could bring this whole thing down around us."

"Is that what you're concerned about?"

"Isn't it enough?"

"I thought perhaps you just didn't want me going riding with any man who's not named Page Murdock."

"That door closed in Breen."

"Doors have been known to open."

She went through one then, leaving me alone on the boardwalk with the cedar chief.

## 12

"No, no, *Señor* Murdock. *Es imposible.* It cannot be done."

"Why not?" I said. "He's wanted for the stickup at the Apache Princess. You identified him yourself."

Rosario Ortiz shook his head. I wasn't sure if it was at the prospect of getting up a posse to track down Ross Baronet or the determination of the stalk of feathergrass he was grasping in both hands to hang on to its place among his yellow roses. He had on his gardening outfit of overalls, army coat, and sombrero, and the effort had him red and sweating. In truth I couldn't picture the fat part-time lawman at the head of a mounted party of armed men.

"To begin with, he is by now among the caves in Chihuahua. They are a honeycomb and have been known to swallow a platoon of cavalry for a week."

"You don't know he's there. You're only guessing."

"In the second place, he has nothing that belongs to you. You have the lives of two of his *compañeros*, in fact. If anyone should be hunting anyone, it is he who should be hunting you. But you see he is not. This is because he is a man of reason."

"Tell me, does that star the city gave you mean anything?"

"*Sí, señor*." He gave one last tug. The stalk tore loose suddenly, leaving the root below the ground. He bared his teeth at the fragment in his hand, threw it aside, and sat back on his heels to take off the sombrero and drag a sleeve across his eyes. "It means five dollars a week and ten cents for every rat and stray dog I shoot in the city. Upon this and what I am paid for my work as a carpenter I put clothes on the backs and tortillas in the stomachs of eleven children. *Por favor*, look around you, *señor*. Do you see much carpentry work to be done? Do you see any?"

"Your front door has a broken panel."

"I must be sure and pay myself to replace it. No, *señor*, San Sábado is not Socorro City. A man can live on the rats he shoots there. Here he must clean cisterns and hang doors and make repairs at the mission. He would sweep the floor there as well, except that is Yaquí work and if they catch him at it they will wait for him outside and cut his throat when he leaves. Having told you all this, I hope that you will excuse me if I do not spring into the saddle to run after a bandit who has not stolen anything."

"The families of eight Mexican muleskinners may not agree with that last part."

He crossed himself. "*Lo siento*, it was an infamous

thing. But it is not my concern officially. That incident took place outside this jurisdiction. If I were to go after these swine, who would pay for the provisions?"

"The Apache Princess will, along with a fee for your time."

"Your pardon, *Señor* Murdock." He unfurled a lash of Spanish at a miniature version of himself urinating against the wall of the house at the end of the flower bed. The boy buttoned his fly hastily and ran inside, tears on his face. Ortiz sighed. "You have children, yes?"

"None I know about."

"They are a treasure and a trial. If you spare the rod they will grow up to disappoint you. So will they if you employ it overmuch. These things I suppose are obvious. What is not so obvious is how little is too little, and how much is too much. This business of keeping the peace is simpler by far. I am told you were once a lawman, *es verdad*? You nod. Then you know that to track a man requires the existence of tracks. The Las Cruces pack train robbery is almost a week old."

"If you're so sure about Chihuahua we can go down there and sniff around."

"You do not know that country. It is not just the caves. The place has sheltered brigands and revolutionaries since the time of the Aztecs. Everyone who lives there is either a bandit or the great-great-grandson of one, and strangers are their enemies. Have you ever seen a man cut to pieces by a machete?"

"Sabers, in the war."

"I would not die such a death if it meant the lives of my children and their grandchildren. Chihuahua? No."

"Then what do you suggest?"

"I? Nothing."

"Nothing?"

He shrugged. I've seen all manner of men do that and I'm bound to say no man does it like a Mexican. "You have kept the peace. We may act only when the peace has been broken."

"That's no good. Ross Baronet just made off with six thousand in silver. A man can stay underground a long time on far less."

"I see. You are in a *hurry* to apprehend this man whose actions have cost you nothing."

This time I shrugged, not as well. "If you like you can call it a defensive maneuver. He isn't accustomed to failing, and we did cost him two men. I doubt he's Christian enough to turn the other cheek."

"Your reasons are your own, *señor*. I am not refusing your offer. I cannot make adobe without mud."

I said nothing for a long time. I despised him thoroughly, not so much for his sloth as for the bare fact that he was right. I suppose I hated Judge Blackthorne too, for his deadline, but I was so accustomed to hating him I gave it no thought.

"How can I get word to Don Segundo del Guerrero that I want to see him?" I asked.

He nodded, as if he'd expected the question. "His foreman, Miguel Axtaca, is sometimes at the Mare's Nest Friday night. He has a favorite there, Clara California."

"I know Clara. Axtaca doesn't sound Spanish."

"It is not. It is Indian, very old Indian. He claims kinship with Montezuma the Great."

"I guess it's too much to expect him to have forgiven us Cortez."

"It is difficult to picture Miguel Axtaca forgiving anyone anything, including himself."

"Friday night?"

"When he is not attending to ranch business." His eyes followed me as I got to my feet. "A word of caution, *Señor* Murdock. He is never without friends."

"Do these friends carry machetes?"

"*Por supuesto,*" he said. "Of course. It is a dangerous land."

Colleen was playing a hand of patience when I returned to the Princess. Her morning tea steamed at her elbow in a blue china cup on a saucer. I asked Irish Andy for coffee and he went into the back room for the pot.

"No kibitzing," she said when I brought my cup over and sat down opposite her. "It's a game for one but everybody seems to have an opinion about how it should be played."

"You needn't worry. I've never played it."

She paused in the middle of placing a black four on a red five. "Never?"

"The use of it escapes me. What have you won when you've beaten yourself?"

"Fifteen or twenty fewer minutes between you and the grave. That's where we're all headed anyway."

"Speak for yourself."

"You speak like a man with a system."

"You don't win with a system," I said. "You have to beat the system to win. You're born, you grow up, you settle down, you have children, you die. Being born is something you have no control over, but if you avoid any or all of those in the middle you stand a better than even chance of avoiding the last."

"Don't tell me. You chose not growing up." She turned over the king of hearts.

"I considered it. In the end I decided that playing games to live was for other people."

"Instead you played with guns."

"That wasn't play."

"Wasn't it?"

I met her blue stare. "No."

"Perhaps not." She went bust and gathered in the cards. "I heard you had trouble with Indians."

"They had all the trouble. Jubilo told me he picked up the papers for Frank Baronet. Did you write them up the way we discussed them?"

"Yes. Don't you trust your partners?"

"I trust Junior."

"You would. He's a man."

"He hasn't gone riding with Eille MacNutt."

She shuffled the deck the way she never did with rubes present, watching me over the blur. "Why don't you say what you mean? You're not concerned over any trouble with the Mare's Nest in connection with our business arrangement. You wouldn't be if Junior had proposed it."

I sat back, grinning over my coffee. Irish Andy had faded away at the beginning of the conversation. A discreet Prussian is a rare beast. He was undoubtedly listening from the back room.

"You know, I think I like you better when you're not smiling," Colleen said. "It makes you look hydrophobic."

"There's no help for it. I never met a woman who looked to her clothes and face and hair the way a gun man looks to his weapons and didn't complain about how every man she spoke to wanted to bed her. I think about that and before you know it my teeth are showing."

She fanned the deck. "I think you mix up comment with complaint."

"Who gave you the ring?"

"Who did you go to see in Laramie?"

I sipped from my cup. The conversation was becoming dangerous.

"Quiet morning," I said.

"They are all quiet. It's my favorite time of day in a saloon, when the air is still clear and the glasses are all polished and twinkling and the man behind the bar is crisp with starch and means it when he says welcome. Before the punchers and the miners and the tumbleweed tinhorns blow in all stinking of horse and lime water and the air fills with smoke and noise and stale beer. From heaven to hell in the space of a few minutes."

"You seem to handle it well enough when they line up at your table."

"It's the old conflict." She turned over the cards with a rippling movement of one finger and they were all black. "What you do to live versus what you live to do." She rippled them the other way, and now they were all red.

"You won't live long if you do that in front of the customers."

"Since the only customer in the room just passed out in the middle of the free lunch I would say the point is moot. In any case when they come in this early, it isn't cards they're desperate for."

"How shall we kill time until the rush?" I asked.

"There is always blackjack."

"Not with your deck."

"I haven't marked a card in four years," she said. "I am too good to have the need."

"The last three card-markers I shot all said the same thing. I have a deck upstairs."

She did the trick with the reds and blacks one last time, then stacked them and smoothed the edges. "I'll help you find it."

Upstairs, in the half-light edging in around the crooked window shade, I managed all her hooks and buttons but had trouble with the stays, which she undid herself with a deft movement. She had put on weight since the last time, but not much, and she wore it well. We started out awkward and unsure, and the feather mattress was no improvement on the one in Breen, but we found the middle ground together and she cried out softly, once. Later she watched me open the bundle that had come on the stage and put on the new shirt and the suit of clothes I'd had made to my measurements before leaving Helena. The coat was a simple charcoal-gray frock with stepped lapels from which I'd had the black satin facing removed on the same principle that prevented me from wearing a star, to avoid drawing fire. The only other adjustment involved a double-reinforced inside breast pocket designed to carry the Deane-Adams. In the wavy mirror over the basin the sober material lay flat across my shoulders like a good saddle blanket. The trouser cuffs broke at the insteps of my boots and the low-cut vest hugged my ribs without constricting them when I moved. This attention to movement was remarkable on the part of this particular tailor, who had an exclusive contract with Judge Blackthorne's court to provide burial clothes for officers slain in the line of duty. It was probably the first suit he'd made in years that didn't fasten loosely up the back.

"What's your opinion?" I tugged at the hem of the coat and adjusted the string tie. I could load a revolver in the dark with my teeth but I couldn't tie a cravat straight to preserve the Union.

"It's wrinkled in back. You should have hung it up as soon as it arrived."

"The sleeves are too short. I told him not to show more than an inch and a half of cuff."

"No, two inches is what they were showing the last time I visited Saint Louis."

"I look like a crooked banker."

"The suit isn't *that* good."

"Aside from all that."

"Do you need a compliment that badly?"

"I need truth. If I were going out after someone for the first time I'd ask someone who knew about it if I had everything I needed. I never ran a saloon before."

She was sitting up in bed with the counterpane tucked under her arms, resting a hand with a cheroot smoldering between two fingers on one raised knee.

With her black hair undone she looked younger, girl-
ish. "Not bad for an aging mankiller," she said.

"I mean the suit."

A pillow whipped past my head and flattened
against the door, coughing feathers out a burst seam.
"Clear out while I get dressed."

"I'll wait for you outside."

"Why?"

"You won't let me wait inside."

She took in smoke and didn't let any out. "This
didn't signify anything. Breen's an empty spot along
the U.P. right-of-way. So is everything that happened
there. It's not even history."

"I didn't hear myself proposing."

"That's just as well. Whatever you think of me, I
only marry one man at a time." She threw the cheroot at the basin and slid out of bed, stark naked.
"Make sure the latch catches."

Junior was behind the bar in his shirtsleeves when
we entered the Princess a few minutes later. He
looked at us and said, "Well, I'm glad there's one man
in town doesn't depend on the Mare's Nest for his
entertainment."

# 13

I DON'T KNOW why even now, but somehow I knew Miguel Axtaca wouldn't be at Eille MacNutt's place that Friday night. Probably it was my lack of faith in my good fortune. I went there anyway, and stretched half a bottle of gin over three hours listening to Mac-Nutt's mulatto pianist making a hash of Gilbert and Sullivan on an upright someone had salvaged from a wagon trail and buying the occasional drink for Clara California and Adabelle. The latter was easily the least resistible of the string, five feet and eighty-two pounds, most of it bust, in a tight shift with nothing but perfume between it and her, and short coppery hair that hugged her head like a bright helmet. If she was as frigid as Clara claimed, there was a thaw on that night; she accidentally brushed my arm with her breast at least a dozen times and insisted on cleaning up the debris by hand after she upended a dish of hard candies into my lap. She was either dedicated to her work or the clumsiest woman I'd seen in a long time.

The place was finished off with flocked wallpaper over plaster and complicated further with framed steelpoint engravings of nymphs and satyrs going about their traditional business in pastoral settings and embroidered pillows scattered among the skirted sofas and lamps with fringed shades. MacNutt made no appearance. The responsibility of greeting customers fell to a small, straight-backed woman in a plain gray dress buttoned to the throat and her hair in a bun who shielded her weak eyes behind rectangular spectacles with tinted lenses. I hadn't seen her before, but this was my first time inside the establishment during business hours, and when she introduced herself as Phyllis MacNutt I assumed she was the proprietor's sister, although it developed in conversation later that she was his wife. What she thought about her husband going riding with someone like Colleen Bower was well concealed behind those opaque shards of glass.

I got out of there around eleven with what was left of my virtue intact. I spent the next week letting my new suit grow acquainted with my angles and hollows while I dealt faro and spelled Irish Andy behind the bar and took Colleen upstairs twice. Neither the gold ring she wore nor the reason for my trip to Laramie came up again. Both times she was affectionate and eager, but with the exception of a good poker reader like Junior Harper anyone who saw us together downstairs would have thought we were no more than partners.

And he'd have been right. Whatever intangible

thing that had existed between us in Breen was as gone as that town itself, torn up along with the timbers and siding when the economic balance shifted and transported farther down the line in the hands of strangers. Taking her to bed was like playing a friendly game of cards with someone you once had much in common with and don't anymore; then the cards were just an excuse, and now it was just the cards.

And September crept along in its sluggish way, growing golden everywhere but in that desert climate, where the days melded together without a seam and everything was the color of adobe and dried blood.

On the second Friday I reported to the Mare's Nest just as the last rusty streamer was spiraling down behind the Cristobals; and I knew as soon as I opened the door, before my eyes adjusted to the dim interior, that he was there. A pungent mix of old sweat—layers of it dried in separate sheets—and open-air woodsmoke abraded my nostrils. It was a stink I knew well and had worn often enough myself, the kind that accompanies men who haven't spent a day under a roof in weeks.

I spotted them over Phyllis MacNutt's shoulder, three men seated in kitchen chairs along the back wall facing the door and passing a bottle of mescal back and forth. Clara California was sitting on the floor near the one in the middle with her feet gathered under her, stroking her cheek with his left hand.

Three identical pairs of obsidian eyes observed my approach. "Miguel Axtaca?"

The question floated like a feather descending a mine shaft. Then the man on the left spoke. "Who is asking?"

I gave him my attention briefly. He was thick through the torso in a white peasant shirt and canvas trousers with an ammunition belt slung slantwise across his left shoulder. The man on the right was dressed the same, and the two looked enough alike to be brothers. Both had large brown faces scored all over, shaggy moustaches, and masses of black oily hair that they combed straight back with their fingers, the tracks of which showed as clearly as furrows in fresh loam. Their machetes leaned against the wall beside their chairs, thonged grips close to hand.

"Page Murdock." I was addressing the man in the center. "I'm part owner of the Apache Princess down the street."

He said nothing. There wasn't anything Spanish about him. He was lean for a Mexican in his middle years and his features resembled primitive architecture. A block of brow rested like a lintel on the thick post of his nose, his mouth slicing straight across underneath. He wore his black hair in bangs chopped off square above the eyes. The rest stopped just short of his shoulders, as coarse as broomstraw. His costume matched those of his companions except for the lack of a cartridge belt or any other indication that he carried a weapon of any kind. That was worrisome. I knew he had one, I just didn't know what it was or where he kept it. A man who arms himself in secret is a man who will come at you from behind.

And there was something else. I'd dismissed that claim of descendancy from Montezuma as an empty boast; now I wasn't so sure. I had always heard Aztecs were extinct, but once when Judge Blackthorne had kept me waiting in his chambers I saw a woodcut in one of his thumb-blurred books showing ancient Indians greeting the Conquistadores, and Miguel Axtaca was the closest thing to them I'd encountered. Indians in general are easy to read, but whatever thoughts were going on behind that crudely hewn face were as hidden as his weapon.

"We do our drinking here." Evidently the Mexican on the left was the spokesman for the group.

"I'm not here to drum up business. I have something to discuss with *Señor* Axtaca."

"No *señor*." This from the man himself, in a voice that grated from disuse. "Just Axtaca. Miguel to my friends. What do you wish to discuss?"

"It's private."

"Everything is private with you white men. Then you whisper it in the ears of your whores and it is known all over."

"It's about Ross Baronet."

"I have heard this name and so have these men. Speak if you will speak."

"It's really for your boss. I want to meet with him to discuss bringing Ross Baronet to justice."

"Mexico is a republic where all men are free. You may go there and see him. My permission is not necessary."

"That's not how it works," I said. "Not in your country, and not in mine. It's supposed to but it's not. Where and when can I meet with him?"

The man on the right spoke for the first time. His Spanish was too rapid for me to follow. Axtaca replied more slowly in a dialect I had never run across before. The conversation took place with neither of them taking their eyes off me. I felt like something on the auction block.

The foreman switched back to English. "We go from here tomorrow at first light. You may come or not. We will not wait."

"How far is it to the ranch?"

"You are on it now."

I wanted to pursue that one, but he exerted pressure on Clara California's hand and she rose from the floor and climbed onto his lap, and I decided the interview was over. I took my leave.

"Old Don Segundo's got a bug up his ass about San Sábado," Junior said when I joined him at the Princess, where he was drinking his nightly glass of hot water before retiring. "His great-great-granddaddy or somebody got five million acres from King Ferdinand for burning heretics or somesuch and no Mexican War is going to change his conviction that we're all of us squatting."

"Give a man a grant for all eternity and he will take it seriously every time," I said. "Does he do anything about it besides write angry letters to Santa Fe?"

"Fifteen years ago he got up his own army and led it into the field for Juárez. He had three horses shot out from under him at Santillo. They say he is still known down there as the White Lion. Then when the new president had the *cojones* to tax him he backed the Díaz revolution. That came close to busting him when it fell apart, but when Juárez died and Díaz came to power the old bastard found himself right welcome in Mexico City. They say he personally hung better than a hundred men for rustling his stock before he lost the use of his legs. Then he got surly.''

"What happened to his legs?"

"Horse fell on him or something. I guess he learned you don't go around busting remudas past seventy, but I wouldn't count on it. He's a stubborn old cob. What makes him so interesting all of a sudden?''

"I ran into his foreman tonight at the Mare's Nest.''

His forehead creased. "You talked to Miguel Axtaca?''

"If you can call it that. He is no conversationalist.''

"He's a savage is what he is. He sacrifices goats and the reason he only sacrifices goats is Don Segundo was running out of vaqueros. Clara California's the only whore in MacNutt's string will go with him. She's as crazy as a duck that flies backwards. What would you have to talk about with Miguel Axtaca?''

"He's taking me to see the old man tomorrow at daybreak.''

He had started to raise his glass. Now he set it down. "You looking for cattle work? I can tell you now, I've had a bet with Colleen since the day you left to go talk to the sheriff that you wouldn't last six months in the saloon business, but I thought it was marshaling you'd go back to. I was sure you had your fill of leather on the hoof a long time ago.''

"Colleen bet I'd stay with saloon work?''

"She couldn't pass up the odds. If you miss ranching so much, what's wrong with working for John Whiteside? He's American and the climate beats old Mexico."

"I wouldn't go back to the cattle trade for a Yankee dollar. I thought you knew me better than that."

"I know you good enough to know when you don't answer a question it means you don't like the question any better than I'm fixing to like the answer."

Irish Andy had stopped polishing glasses. I sat forward and lowered my voice. "I'm going after Ross Baronet. I figure the only man in the area who wants him more than I do is the old don. I'm hoping he'll help me outfit a posse."

He grasped my forearm suddenly. The tensile strength in Junior's fingers always came as a surprise to those who shook hands with him. "Page, he didn't get anything from the Princess. Two of his men dead is what he got. What are you out to prove?"

"You wouldn't understand it. It doesn't make any sense. I never stood still for a stickup all the time I rode for Blackthorne. The only difference is this time I'm riding for myself."

"Maybe you forgot he's Frank Baronet's brother. Apart from the fact he's our new partner, this is his county. You calculate he's going to just sit there on his fancy pillow while you ride Ross down?"

"I'm curious to see just what he does. He's on record as having Ross dead and buried in Mexico. His constituents might fall to wondering what he stands to gain by protecting a corpse."

"You know what I think? I think he don't care what his constituents think. I think if it's you or his brother he'll pick his brother a hundred times out of a hundred, dead or alive. You're my friend and I'll miss you, but this don't figure to stop with you. This here is the first chance I've had since my old man died to show I pump Harper blood. I'm not about to lose it on account of you can't remember you handed in your papers. Don't do this thing, Page."

"It might not pan out. If it does, Marshal Ortiz has agreed to head up the posse. It's every citizen's duty to help out when the peace is broken."

"Ortiz couldn't head up an expedition to locate his fat ass. Baronet's going to know who's in charge."

"I'm not asking your permission, Junior. I'm just letting you know what's in the wind so you'll be prepared. If the sheriff comes around looking for answers, tell him you don't know where I've gone."

"I kind of hoped my last words would have a better ring."

"He's not going to hurt you or the Princess. He's not going to do anything that will jeopardize his investment."

"That's what you had in mind when you brought him up, isn't it?" he said. "You had this worked out even before Ross hit the place. What's your game, Page? It sure isn't poker."

"I'll tell you what it is."

Colleen Bower had closed her faro game and seen off her last customer. Now she swung a chair out from the table next to ours and sat down. She had a black choker around her throat with a green stone that drew the eye down the front of her dress and away from the cards. The pupils of her eyes glittered as large and bright as dimes—the application of belladonna without causing instant death is an art—and her hair was arranged in sausage curls the way it was the first time we met, two summers and a thousand years ago. Irish Andy was there immediately with the cup of tea she favored when her work was done. The big squarehead had a crush on her the size of Düsseldorf.

When he had withdrawn she said, "Being the law, that's Mr. Murdock's game."

"I admit I have a turn for it," I said. "I thought I could quit cold, but maybe I can taper off. There's always a call for men to ride posse."

"I don't mean it's in your blood. I mean it's your game. The same game you've been playing since before we met. You're still playing it."

"Get it out of your craw, Colleen," Junior said. "I'd have been married before this if I could just find a woman who says what she means the first time."

"I mean the reason Murdock can't stop being a marshal is he never stopped." She opened her reticule, removed a travel-worn fold of familiar-looking yellow paper, and spread it out on the table. YOU LEFT YOUR WALKING STICK IN HELENA, it read. "Next time you leave a woman alone in your room with all your things, think about emptying your pockets first."

# ∾ 14 ∾

"WALKING STICK?" JUNIOR looked lost.

"Blackthorne," said Colleen. "You men are always playing games with codes and symbols, as if no one could see through them with half an eye. That telegram was sent the same day you wired us you were on your way to Laramie to look at a piano. That piano wears black robes and swings a gavel. It makes sense. It never did that you left Judge Blackthorne. The only way it does is you never left him to begin with. If this were wartime, you'd be hanged for a spy. I'm not so sure you still won't be. I'm just wondering who is going to be standing in line behind you on the scaffold."

I said, "That's a good deal to draw from an old piece of paper."

Quick as thought she drew the pocket Remington from the holster inside her reticule, cocking it in the same motion. I could see grains of dust inside the barrel. Not many; she took as good care of her weapon as she did her clothes and her cards and herself. "Junior, if I shoot him and testify he was pressing his attentions upon me, will you side me at the inquest?"

I said, "You're forgetting Irish Andy."

"Andy would side me if I shot Bismarck."

That was true enough. With the shotgun I had used on Dutch Tim well inside his reach the big German was standing with both hands on the bar and that cow-eyed look you saw on young girls gazing at a rotogravure of Edwin Booth. Not much help there. The Deane-Adams was just as inaccessible with a two-inch-thick tabletop between it and my hands. Jack Rimfire could retire on such a fix. Move over, *Satan's Sixgun*. Make room for *The She-Devil of San Sábado*. The cover would feature Sylvia Starr in form-fitting buckskins with a Colt in each comely hand.

"Junior?" I said.

"Is it true, Page?"

That startled me. His narrow face looked young, the lower lip pushed out slightly and his eyes as big as poker chips. I didn't open my mouth. I didn't have any words for it.

"We go back some," he said. "I shot a Nez Percé off his pony with a long gun when he was coming at you with a war club, and you up to your hips in river mud with a calf in your arms and your back turned to boot. You done as good for me a couple of times. I didn't ask you down here to partner me because I needed your gun. I done it because we're friends. Anyway that's what I thought."

"We're still friends."

He shook his head. "I don't know what we are,

but friends sure ain't it. I don't know who you're after or why and I don't care. I hope you get him and it's worth it." He pushed back his chair and stood. "Shoot out a lamp if you don't want to put that pistol up cold. If you was going to shoot him you'd of done it before this." He went out.

"He's got a point." I held out a hand.

This time Colleen shook her head. "Firearms cost money. You lawmen are always taking them off people and never giving them back. It's no wonder there are coming to be so many of you out here. You can eat for the rest of your life on what you make off the resale." She seated the hammer and returned the revolver to her purse. "I shot a police officer in the lip in El Paso. I might as well have finished him for all the yell they put up about it. I've got a policy against running foul of the law twice in one season or you'd be colder than my tea."

"Why the lip?"

"I was aiming between his eyes but the floor was slanted. What kind of errand are you running for Blackthorne?"

"We haven't established I'm running any kind of errand."

"I know it's not me. I haven't shot any federals lately. A stray card or two isn't worth your train fare. Anyway you didn't know I was going to hook up with the Princess. *I* didn't know until I messed up that policeman's lip." She pushed her tea away untasted. "It's Baronet you're after, isn't it? Frank, not Ross. Bad lawmen always did upset your appetite."

We were speaking too low to be heard from the bar, but I leaned back in my chair and told Irish Andy to go home. I said I'd clean up. He took off his apron, got his mackinaw from the back room, said good-night—more for Colleen's benefit than mine—and went out.

"That wasn't necessary," Colleen said. "You can trust Andy not to carry stories. Not because he's loyal. He just doesn't care."

"That's why I don't trust him." I got up and went behind the bar. Under the top, covered by a mouse-chewed feedbag, was the bottle of sour mash whiskey that Andy ordered special from the distributor every month and kept hidden. I filled two glasses and brought them to the table. When I sat down we touched rims and drank. "When Judge Blackthorne took over in Helena he found a man sitting in the city jail waiting to hang for killing a Wells Fargo express agent during a robbery. The man claimed it was his partner who shot the expressman, but he was the only one caught. After interviewing witnesses, Black-thorne wrote to the president, got him to authorize a new trial, and acquitted the man for lack of evidence. The man's name was Cocker Flynn. You never saw it in a newspaper or a dime novel, but he was the first deputy marshal appointed by Judge Blackthorne and he was the best peace officer I ever knew. Everything I know about the work I either learned from him or didn't and went and found out later he was right."

"I assume this story has a point." Her face was un-readable, her success at cards being in no way depen-dent upon the natural distractions of her person.

"Just that the Judge didn't much care if an outlaw turned lawman, or for that matter a lawman turned outlaw, unless he had something to gain or lose from it. My standards are no different. In any case the situation in Socorro County, New Mexico Territory is of no concern to the federal court in Montana."

"If your aim is to convince me that saloonkeeping is your only interest in San Sábado, you went the long way around the barn for nothing."

"I didn't say that."

She turned her palms to the ceiling. "Call."

I told her then, starting with Harlan Blackthorne's intestines lying on the ground at Monterey and finishing with his vow to avenge the murders of Sergeant Uriah Spooner's son and daughter-in-law by the Baronets. I didn't tell it as well as the Judge, but then he was the kind of man you didn't interrupt, and I had to talk fast to get it in between questions from the other side of the table. When I'd finished, and didn't need it anymore, she gave me silence.

"It doesn't signify," she said finally. "For it to do that, I would have to credit the Iron Jurist with humanity. Everything I've ever heard about him says he pounds that gavel to circulate his blood in place of a heart."

"I'd never play cards with the Judge. But I believe him in this case. No other explanation covers it."

"I hope my taxes are not financing this personal vendetta."

"You never paid a tax in your life."

She took another drink and rolled it around, appreciating it. Most of the stock we sold was best rustled past the tongue like doubtful cattle across a border. "What are you going to do about the Apache Princess?"

"I've been thinking about it. If I apprehend Ross

Baronet I'll no longer require it as a cover. Junior offered to buy me out the day I came. I'll sign over my end and you can reimburse me later, possibly out of Frank's end."

"I cannot believe you think that transaction will go through."

"Why not? There's profit all around. Frank knows a good deal when he sees it and you and Junior might as well have the use of his money for as long as he's at large. Gold itself isn't wicked, only its source."

"When were you going to tell Junior and me about this plan?"

"When Frank and Ross Baronet were standing side by side on the scaffold in Helena."

"The conundrum to me is whether marshaling made you the bastard you are or you took to marshaling because you were born a bastard." There was less heat in this than the words implied; yet there was heat. She finished her whiskey, picked up her purse, and rose. Looking down at me: "You didn't say what happened to the man Flynn."

"A fugitive shot him last year. He died while I was talking to him."

She considered it. "Was that better than the rope? I'm curious about your answer."

"It was later, anyway."

"Serves me right for asking." She started toward the door.

"Where are you headed?"

"*Señora* Castillo's. It's late."

I reached for my hat. "I'll see you get there."

"I have the Remington for that. Your day tomorrow starts early, or have you forgotten?"

I let her go. There's no worse company than an angry woman, unless it's one who is right.

A bluish glow, the kind that edges sharpened steel, limned the broken peaks beyond the Jornada del Muerto when I led the claybank from the livery to the Mare's Nest, where Miguel Axtaca's vaquero companions were slouched against the hitching rail, passing a cheroot back and forth.

In the saffron light of the lamp that had been burning in the front window for as long as I had been associated with the city, they looked even larger than they had the night before, their shadows stretching nearly as far as the boardwalk on the opposite side of the street. I couldn't believe they were just cowboys. They had on last night's clothes—I wouldn't have given odds that they had ever had them off—with the addition of burlap serapes and dull brown sombreros that from the looks of them had held many a horse's fill of water. Their stovepipe boots were caked with dust and from crown to heel the two men were the same dun color with nary an inch of exposed metal to catch the light. Even an Apache would have been hard put to spot them at any distance in the desert. A trio of well-fed sorrels were hitched nearby, loaded down with gear, including water bags and Mexican Winchesters on two of them and the ubiquitous machetes, slung from the saddle rings in special scabbards. The animals all bore the same brand, an inverted *V* inside a square tipped up on one corner.

"*Cuerno Diamante,*" said the more garrulous of the pair when I asked about it. "Diamond Horn. It is the sign of Don Segundo as it was of his father and his father's father, the crest of the Guerrero family, a gift from King Philip at the time of the great Armada."

"The Armada sank, I heard."

For answer he drew deeply on the cheroot and handed it to his partner. They were a sharing party. I swear that after one inhaled the other blew smoke.

Presently Axtaca emerged from the building, carrying what looked like a bundle of sticks eighteen inches long bound in a rawhide wrap with symbols painted on it. He too had thrown a serape on over his peasant dress, but it was more elaborate than those of his fellows, embroidered with a fine design in dusky red that would nonetheless be invisible beyond a hundred yards. He wore no hat, only a plain bandanna around his head. Seeing him upright for the first time I realized he was no taller than I, long of waist but short in the legs and bowed unheroically at the knees, and I might have been reminded of an orangutan I'd seen in a medicine show in Helena but for the overall dignity of his bearing. Without a word or a glance in my direction he tied the bundle across the throat of the saddle belonging to the nearest of the three sorrels, the one that carried neither machete nor rifle, untied the reins, and stepped into leather. The less talkative of the two vaqueros threw away the cheroot and the pair followed his lead.

Straddling the claybank, I thought I recognized the bundle as a distant relative of the medicine bags carried by some of the northern tribes. It was a talisman against mishap and, so far as I could determine, the closest thing to a weapon that Don Segundo's foreman carried on his person. In that rough country he was either the bravest man I'd yet encountered, or the most arrogant.

## 15

IT WAS SEPTEMBER everywhere in America except along the Journey of Death. From the time the molten-copper sun cleared the San Andres, the air grew warmer by the minute. The tiny fiery blossoms that opened to drink the condensed moisture by dark and blazed in the early bright curled in on themselves under the mounting heat and vanished like the stain of breath on glass. My coat and my companions' serapes came off early and went behind our saddles. Within minutes I felt the first pricking drops of sweat where my hat met my forehead. You don't wipe away the first sweat of the day in the desert; you let it cover you in a transparent sheet like thin varnish. Another day, another layer, curing your hide in the salt of your own system until it was as scaly as a lizard's back. You can build a house from the human bones you will find bleaching in the desert, but you won't see a gila monster's skeleton.

I was traveling with a silent crew. The most open of the three would have been considered laconic in any company I had ridden with, and some of those would have made a monastery sound like Independence Day. He at least answered questions, although the pauses before his responses were long enough for me to forget what I had asked. The others were as stony as the buttes that appeared and began to multiply as we moved farther south, and he was too polite to reply to a comment not addressed to him directly. His name was Francisco. He took pains to point out that it was not to be shortened to Pancho, Saint Francis having some specific importance to his family whose nature I wasn't able to draw out of him. As I'd suspected, the other vaquero was his brother, younger by ten months, called Carlos. The surname was a mix of Spanish and Indian I could neither pronounce nor remember. They had come to work for Don Segundo when the counterrevolution against Juárez failed, having fought for it with machetes, loyalty, and little else in some backwater of Mexico's remotest province so wild it appeared as only a blank on the best maps. Miguel Axtaca had accompanied them, or rather they him, and it was clear from the outset that their pledge was to him and that he held a position in their regard somewhere between *El Cristo* and the old gods. They would no sooner depart from his course than two drops of water would leave the Bravo to start their own river.

By midday I had begun to think fondly of the winter I had spent in a dugout in the Rockies trapped under twenty feet of snow, wondering if I would have enough toes left to walk out when the thaw came.

The sun was a white coin nailed to a naked sky, and when the hot wind gusted I felt the glue that held my joints together drying out and cracking. Even the claybank hung its vain head. I stopped twice to give it water from my cupped hand and to take some for myself, but the others kept riding without touching their water bags. I'd heard tales of Apaches and their mounts subsisting on sun and dust and nothing else and had charged them to the same kind of frontier storytelling that had grangers in windy Wyoming feeding their chickens buckshot to keep them from blowing away, but here were three men who could outparch any of those mythical Indians. I hadn't felt this far out of my class since the day I tracked a white scalphunter into a railroad owners' banquet in Denver.

When night came we camped south of Las Cruces, where the others watered at last, built a small fire for warmth, and handed around twists of jerked beef. They didn't offer me any and I didn't ask. From the outset it was clear I was just someone who happened to be going in the same direction they were, and if I expired for lack of provisions or water, the occurrence had no more to do with them than the czar's assassination. I opened a tin, ate sardines, drank the juice, and wished for coffee.

The next day was more of the same, with the addition of a few new flat spots on my body thanks to a night spent on the hard earth. If I was adjusting to the heat, that heat was yesterday's; we were nearing the border now and the oven of Chihuahua. Already the scenery looked alien, dotted with plants and bushes I had no name for and corrugated like a brown ocean frozen in mid-roll. And I felt something undefined, an inner caution born of being foreign and alone.

I noticed a change in my companions as well, but in the opposite direction. As we continued south, some of the tension seemed to go out of their posture and they began to look around, not so much in the way of a small party expecting trouble as of travelers noting the changes and samenesses in country they called home. Now they talked among themselves in that boundary mix of Spanish, English, and Indian, and once one of them laughed, a deep open male guffaw that said as clearly as if I understood the language that some mention had been made of a woman. I knew then, from my position not only outside their circle but outside the great vast space that their circle now encompassed, something of how these three men and all their kind felt when they crossed the border heading north.

Somewhere during that trip—I think it was the third day, shortly after we broke camp at the base of a dead volcano still steeped in the stench of sulfur—I turned over another year. I wondered how many other forty-year-old men were still traversing unknown territory on horses that hated them in the company of men who would never be their friends. It seemed that by the halfway point a fellow should have more to his name than he can carry away in two hands.

That afternoon we struck Indian.

There had been signs, although no more than one would expect of a people who drifted along the ground like chaff, leaving little behind to prove they existed: a thread of smoke scratching a faded excla-

mation point against naked sky, a wrinkle of movement atop a distant butte. It was a big country but not
as empty as it looked, and they had been there long
enough to know when something as unnatural as
Man interrupted the pattern of its days. Tiny fleeting
impressions of activity, and then they were there, fifteen of them strung out in a ragged line across an
open space without sufficient cover nearby to conceal
a moccasin. It was a trick I'd have given much to
learn, but I suspected it wasn't something that can be
taught, only known.

Of course they were Apaches, as ugly and toadlike
as the terrain they ruled. Naked but for breechclouts,
they sat hollow-hipped pintos and carried Springfield
rifles with the barrels upright, some of them trailing
feathers from the ends. It was a lot of firepower in one
place for a tribe with nothing worth trading. This was
no ordinary raiding party, I decided, but an escort of
some kind. As unobstrusively as possible I reached
behind my saddle and loosened the Winchester in its
scabbard.

There was no movement on their side except for
their mounts' nervous heads and the wind stirring
their hair, unfettered and without decoration. A mile
above them an eagle—I hoped superstitiously it
wasn't a vulture—hung suspended from its broad
wings, painted there. The three Mexicans conferred.
Then Miguel Axtaca kneed his sorrel forward. In one
hand he held his reins high while he lifted the other
with the palm out to show he had no weapon. He'd
advanced ten feet when one of the Springfields spoke.

The barrel came down, the butt went up to the
Indian's shoulder, white smoke puffed from the muz-

zle and slid sideways with the wind. Something tugged at the dry earth several yards in front of Axtaca's horse. He drew rein, Francisco and Carlos hoisted their carbines and worked the levers. Six or seven days later the sound of the shot reached us, a hollow *plop* like a frog jumping into a pond. Axtaca dropped his hand and pushed the palm back, stopping the others from returning fire. It had been a warning shot.

At the end of another week the Apache mounted at the center of the line raised one hand and made a sign. After a moment Axtaca responded. Then—it had to be for my benefit—he spoke his first words of English since the night we had met in the Mare's Nest.

"He wants all of us to come."

A pause. The vaqueros lowered their Winchesters.

Once, in Dakota Territory, I'd ridden ninety miles with a Cheyenne arrowhead between my shoulder blades to Yankton and the nearest doctor. The arrowhead was poisoned with toad spume and human manure and I lay for three weeks in delirium. From start to finish the experience wasn't as long as the half-mile we crossed that afternoon. The Apaches made no move to shorten the distance, remaining as impassive as foothills.

When we were about fifty feet apart the Indian in the center barked. A linguist might have made something of the guttural syllable, but it was the closest approximation to the sound a big dog makes when its hackles are standing as I had ever heard from a fellow human. Its meaning was clear enough and we stopped.

During the conversation that ensued, carried on entirely between Miguel Axtaca and the Apache who seemed to be in charge in a language completely unrelated to the one the Aztec had been using for days, I had plenty of opportunity to study the other side. They were all males and mostly young, one or two barely old enough to have passed whatever test for manhood that tribe observed, and in general they were lean almost to the point of emaciation, their rib cages standing out like umbrella staves beneath burnished flesh. Here was a predatory people, half-starved like wolves and therefore dangerous. Many were scarred—one in fact had come close to having his head split open from the way the new hair stood out like quills from a crescent of fresh pink skin on the right side of his head, as wide as the spread fingers of a man's hand. Despite their alien features, the broad flat faces, slit eyes, sharp noses, and mouths like razor cuts, there was about them that grim weary faithless air of the veteran killer that I had breathed in more places than I could count, from Shiloh to Adobe Walls to the massacre at Sand Creek. It observes neither race nor creed and jumps all the barriers between.

All of this and a good deal more was present in their leader. He was easily the oldest of the band, nearly three times the age of its youngest member, with iron gray in his relatively short hair and deep creases crosshatching every square inch of his face. His eyes, small and close-set, smoldered steadily in the deep shadows of his brow like embers in a cave. There was no decency in them, nothing that passed for mercy, no capacity for any emotion but hate.

Somewhere I have a photograph that was taken of him much later at Fort Sill, and after forty years the raw hostility in those eyes has not lessened; it spans the decades like a scar on the land. At the time I had barely heard his name, but its four syllables have come to sum up my experiences in the Great Southwest of 1881 in a way that no whole book or paragraph could.

At one point during the conversation, the Apache gestured toward the medicine bag tied across the pommel of Axtaca's saddle. Don Segundo's foreman touched it with the ends of his thick fingers and said something in a tone softer than any I had heard him use previously. On the other side, the harsh flame in the eyes belonging to the granite head altered, then became pitiless once again. The head nodded slightly. More talk followed, punctuated by hand signs on both sides. At length the line of Indians turned, collapsing upon itself like a cotton clothesline, and moved off toward the east. Not one of the riders looked back.

"What did he say to them?" I asked Francisco. I was sure some trick was involved. The Apaches knew no prayer but Death to the Enemy, and they had no enemy they despised worse than Mexicans. Since 1840 the State of Chihuahua had issued a bounty of one hundred dollars for each male Apache scalp and fifty for each female.

Francisco rearranged his thick shoulders. "I do not speak Apache."

Axtaca turned in his saddle and fixed his obsidian gaze on me. He had neither looked at me nor acknowledged my existence since San Sábado. In that desert glare his face looked like something shaped by erosion.

"I lived with the Chiricahua Apaches from the time I was six until I turned fourteen," he said. "I am the only man not a Chiricahua who is allowed to display their symbol upon my traps. I know the secret name of God. Geronimo is a Chiricahua. All these things I told him and he wished me good medicine on my journey."

"That was Geronimo?"

"It is the name by which the Mexicans and the Americans know him. I addressed him by his warrior name, which your *norteamericano* tongue could never manage." He pitied me that.

"I thought he'd be taller," I said.

## ⤳ 16 ⤳

WITH TWO HOURS of light remaining we passed a long-
horn skull polished white and set on a flat piece of
shale. The Diamond Horn brand had been burned
into its forehead above letters in faded red paint reading PROHIBIDA LA ENTRADA. It was the only indication
that we had entered the region acknowledged by two
governments to belong to Don Segundo del Guerrero,
the White Lion of Chihuahua. Here and there across
that rocky plain, knots of surly beeves stood around
munching the short tough grass that did nothing to
fill out their hollow hips and exposed ribs.

Another hour went by before we came within
sight of ranch headquarters, an adobe oblong with a
thatched roof and the long veranda unique to the
Spanish gentry, as if shade itself were the special
property of the wealthy. But for that it might have
been any one of a thousand such structures you saw
down there and scarcely noted. Whatever preten-

sions the old man might have inherited from his noble ancestors had apparently been leeched from him by the dirty stuff of revolution.

We dismounted before the porch and tied up at the rail. My legs felt as stiff as uncured leather. One of those yellow dogs of indeterminate breed that proliferate in that country lifted its chin from its paws on an ancient glider, growled, and went back to sleep. Its coat was tattered with mange and glittered with flies.

The front door was opened by a bell-shaped woman in a print blouse and a dark skirt whose hem swept the floor. Her gray hair was caught with combs behind her head, tight enough to pull the creases out of her face, which held no expression. I assumed she was the housekeeper, but at sight of her the two vaqueros removed their hats and Miguel Axtaca addressed her as *Señora* Guerrero. On further study I realized too that she was a good deal younger than she at first appeared. That raw land was full of women whose youth had been burned away by the struggle to survive both the climate and the force of their men's character.

After a brief exchange in Spanish, and with barely a glance at me, she stood aside and we entered. Francisco and Carlos paused to cross themselves before an impressive carved wooden crucifix mounted on the wall opposite the door, but Axtaca went on through the shallow room and out the open door on the other side.

It was a pleasant room, running nearly the length of the house and elegantly furnished in contrast to the building's exterior. There were bright rugs on the oiled floor, tasteful religious paintings in ornate frames, camelback sofas upholstered in wine-colored velvet, and silver everywhere, twinkling in the late-afternoon light sliding through the small curtained windows. The place was well ventilated and notice-ably cooler than the veranda. That was its chief lux-ury and the thing that spoke loudest of the old don's position in the community.

Outside, a shot rang out.

The vaqueros and I caught up with the foreman on a back porch as long as the one in front just as another report sounded. There, a very old man in a wicker wheelchair with a Hopi rug spread across his lap sat at a long bench facing the open plain. In spite of the heat he had on a heavy brick-colored sweater with a shawl collar and all its buttons fastened and a straw hat that had seen all its best years, sunlight dap-pling his face through gaping holes in the broad floppy brim. His hair was white, startlingly so against the deep brown of his skin, curling over his collar, and he wore the spade-shaped Castilian beard and a pair of those elaborate moustaches that required suspen-sion in a special hammock when their owners slept; trimmed, waxed, and coiled at the ends. His long hands were spotted and clawlike, but the fingers were dextrous as he laid a rifle with a long brass barrel on the bench and accepted another from the man stand-ing at his side. There were eight rifles lined up on the bench, including three Hawkens, a Sharps, a pair of large-bore Remingtons, a Springfield, and a foreign make I couldn't identify. They were all single-shot and long-range. Sharpshooter's guns.

The ungainly hands, shriveled and plainly rheu-matic, came alive when they gripped a rifle—in this case the Springfield—drew back the breech to inspect the load, and slammed it home. Resting his elbows on the bench, he socketed the buttstock in the hollow of his right shoulder and sighted down the barrel with both eyes open. The rifle pulsed when he squeezed the trigger, but his grip remained as steady as a sunken post. He said, "Bah!" and laid the Springfield next to the gun with the brass barrel.

The man standing next to him lifted and proffered one of the Hawkens. This was a plain-faced Mexican nearly his age, but in full possession of his legs, dressed in sandals and the white cotton uniform of the peasantry. He had a fringe of white hair around a bald head and a pair of moustaches that had never known a hammock, drooping like tired wings to cover his mouth and chin. Houseboys come in all ages.

Don Segundo—the old man in the wheelchair could be no other—was raising the Hawken to firing position when Axtaca cleared his throat.

"*Sí*, Miguel." The don fired. I searched for his target but could detect nothing worth spending ammunition on as far as the Sierra Madres. I had been to Mexico before and had never seen anything to equal the price of an ounce of powder in the entire country; but that was just me. People as different as Cortéz, Louis Napoleon, and Montezuma the Great had chosen to gamble their fortunes on the place without taking me into their confidence.

An exchange of Spanish followed between rancher and foreman, too rapid for me to catch anything beyond an occasional reference to cattle, while the old man inspected the Hawken's hammer, working it back and forth. Apparently he was taken with the rifle. At length he laid it aside and sat back, fixing me from under the ruined straw brim with eyes as blue and clear as matched terrestrial globes. *"¿Y usted?"* It was less a question than a command.

*"No español, jefe."* It was the only phrase I'd acquired that had any use for me.

"A grave error. In my eighty-one years I have spent a total of only six months in your country, and yet I took the trouble to learn the rudiments of the language."

His accent was heavy, but I suspected this was due not so much to ignorance as to lack of practice.

"My range is Montana Territory," I said. "I'm a good deal closer to Canada than I am to Mexico." I told him my name.

It meant nothing to him. "Are you a hunting man, *Señor* Murdock?"

"Elk, a little. And men."

"Man, bah! As quarry he is truly overrated. He lacks instinct. His senses are inferior to the armadillo's, who flees his own shadow. There is no sport in hunting men."

"I never did it for sport."

He didn't pursue it. "Lions are the thing. You begin by hunting them, and if you are not watchful you find that they are hunting you. I have been entreated by tenants of my ranch to bring to an end the marauding ways of a certain cat that lives above the Río Santa María. He is a *viejo*, an old one that eats people because it can no longer outrun antelope. You see by this my meaning when I say that man offers no challenge. I am to prevent it from making away with any more small children."

"That's rough country for a wheelchair."

"The chair is a poor enough substitute for a horse but more easily maneuvered inside a house. I shall of course be mounted. What my legs have forgotten my arms remember. *Quita las otras*, Jesús. I shall use the Hawken."

The old servant gathered the other rifles into his arms and carried them inside. Don Segundo picked up the Hawken, drew a bead on something in the distance, and snapped the hammer on the empty chamber. "Miguel informs me you are on a mission."

"One that may interest you. I want to arrest Ross Baronet and bring him to trial."

"And you have come to ask my permission?"

"For your help. In order to make it official I need the cooperation of the marshal of San Sábado, but he's reluctant. With the support of one such as you I think I can bring him around."

"Refresh an old man's memory, *Señor* Murdock. I have not been across the border in more than forty years. Who is the marshal of San Sábado at present?"

"A man named Rosario Ortiz."

He had been tracking something through the Hawken's sights, sliding the barrel along the horizon. Now he lowered it. "I know this name. What has he to do with the man Baronet? What, for that matter, has *La Ciudad de las Viudas* to do with him? The ambush in which my vaqueros were slain took place near Las Cruces."

"The crime I intend to charge him with is the attempted robbery of the Apache Princess, a saloon in San Sábado."

"How many were slain in this attempt?"

"Two. Both belonged to Baronet."

"I think I understand. *Dinero* takes precedence over eight Mexican lives."

"I didn't say that, sir. Once he's in custody he'll likely be charged with the assault on the pack train, if there's evidence to place him at the scene. My interest is the saloon robbery. I own a one-third interest in the Apache Princess."

The magnificent moustaches twitched. "This I *do* understand. A man protects what is his. Tell me this. What have I to gain from this transaction? I have access to a thousand men at arms. I hardly require the assistance of one gringo and a soft city lawman."

I threw the dice.

"If you thought he was hiding out anywhere in this country, you'd have run him down and strung him up by now, in which case you would have sent me on my way before this. That means he's up north, and you have too many ties with Mexico City to risk sending an armed force across the border and giving the United States Army an excuse to come down here and try out its new Napoleons in a war with Mexico. But with a duly appointed city marshal and a former United States deputy marshal—that's me—riding up front, the entire affair can be represented as a joint action involving two friendly nations equally concerned about the lawlessness along their frontiers. Instead of an invasion, it would be an act of diplomacy."

Miguel Axtaca and the two vaqueros were watching us both through all this. Francisco and Carlos were plainly confused, not so much by my blinding example of logic as by all this English. How much the Aztec was following I couldn't say. He was a stone idol.

"You are a lawyer, *Señor* Murdock?" Don Segundo asked after a long silence. His gnarled old hands were folded atop the long rifle resting across the arms of his wheelchair.

"I rode for the federal court up in Montana Territory for six years. I guess some of that speechifying was bound to rub off."

"You have stated your case well."

Again I waited. Jesús, the manservant, came out carrying a heavy brocaded rug and draped it across the old man's shoulders. The landscape beyond the porch was swimming in heat.

"I invite you to stay here tonight. Dolores is an ordinary cook, but I think you will enjoy her tortillas more than the camp food you have been eating. In the morning I shall tell you what I have decided."

Without waiting for a response, he returned the Hawken to the bench and nodded at Jesús, who turned and pushed him into the house. Axtaca and the vaqueros glanced at me—high praise, but then I had become one of the anointed—and followed.

As a cook, Dolores del Guerrero was Mexico's best-kept secret. Her tortillas were thin enough to read a newspaper through, yet strong enough to hoist a plateful of chili peppers without crumbling, and they melted on contact with the human tongue. The wine was blood-red and strong, poured by Jesús from a green bottle whose label bore the Diamond Horn crest. All the food was served by the woman. Axtaca, who on the trail would have outstarved a Spartan, filled his plate three times and drained the bottle into his glass when the rest of us had had enough. Francisco and Carlos were absent, probably sharing a table with the other vaqueros in the bunkhouse.

The foreman appeared to be a favorite with the woman of the hacienda, who seemed to know no English but was extremely vocal in her native tongue, addressing Axtaca softly but aiming sharp barbs at her husband, whose one small portion of food washed down with plain water was evidently a nightly habit and interpreted by *La Doña* as a comment upon her abilities in the kitchen. By contrast, his responses, if they were responses, sounded conciliatory, even meek. It was clear enough that while the White Lion of Chihuahua held full reign over an area of land larger than the Commonwealth of Massachusetts, the den belonged to his mate. I earned a shy approving smile from her direction by accepting a second helping gratefully.

Jesús gave up his quarters for a cot in the bunkhouse and I passed the night on a straw pallet under a heavy quilt—welcome in the cold of the desert at night—in a tiny room at the end of the house. It was just big enough to contain the pallet and a portable altar with a candle guttering before a miniature painting of the Virgin and Child, inestimably ancient, in a frame three times its size. Outside, coyotes yipped, mourning the loss of the moon. I went to sleep fast and didn't stir until I smelled breakfast cooking.

Someone knocked at the door while I was pulling on my boots. Jesús, looking none the worse for his

night outside the house, entered at my invitation, inclined his head, and informed me in halting English
that Don Segundo requested my presence in his bedroom.

"Thank you, Jesús. I am sorry to have come between you and Mary."

His eyes went to the icon and he crossed himself.
"None can do that, *señor.*" He bowed again and withdrew.

The room, two doors down from the one where I
had slept, was not much larger and filled almost to the
walls by a four-poster of ornate old carved mahogany
with a brightly colored counterpane of native work-
manship folded at the foot. The old man, attired in a
plain linen nightshirt, sat propped against a number
of embroidered pillows with a footed tray across his
lap supporting a thick slice of corn bread and a pot of
steaming coffee. He was pouring some of its contents
into a yellow china cup when I entered. Without the
hat, he displayed a fine head of creamy white hair
brushed straight back behind his ears from a dark
widow's peak. The ends of his moustaches continued
to defy gravity, and I was more sure than ever that he
wore some kind of device to support them while he
slept.

"Breakfast is corn bread and hotcakes with
honey," he said without greeting. "Jesús has a
cousin in Sonora who keeps bees. I cannot abide it
myself. Once you have eaten, Miguel will escort you
as far as El Paso del Norte, where you may cross the
bridge to the American side and ride the stagecoach
from there to San Sábado. Miguel has a way with
the Apaches. They will not harass you."

"You're turning me down?"

"Hear me out before you speak. I am sending you home to make your arrangements with Marshal Ortiz. On the twenty-second of this month you will go to Las Cruces and meet with my vaqueros under Miguel's command. Together you will ride to the place where this dog Baronet is hidden."

"You talk as if you know where that is."

His disconcerting blue eyes nailed me over the rim of the cup.

"But of course. He is with his brother, the sheriff of Socorro County. I supposed everyone knew this."

# ❦ 17 ❦

I'VE DONE A fair amount of traveling in my time, very little of it under ideal conditions. I've frozen in the leaking holds of sailing clippers, sweltered by the fireboxes of tramp steamers, counted the joints in the rails between Dodge City and Abilene on the floor of a cattle car, lashed oxen through blizzards with a wagonload of stoves behind waiting to burst their moorings on the downgrade and crush me like a tick, and rubbed sores in my person on the backs of all manner of horses from racing thoroughbreds to a gunnysack full of bones and bad temper. In 1914 I even took a spin in a kitelike contraption built of sticks and canvas and held together with piano wire that lifted me above the Colorado Rockies and deposited me in a tangle of torn fabric and broken ribs in a place called Fair Play. You could say I've seen the elephant from all five sides. But even in my present extremity I'd choose any one of those methods of transportation over twelve hours in a Butterfield coach.

They called them Bozeman bone-breakers, and for once they weren't exaggerating. The leather straps upon which the body of the vehicle was suspended were designed for the comfort of the horses, not the passengers, and the four of us—a Creole lawyer from New Orleans named Dupont who smelled of trade whiskey and lavender, a grizzle-bearded Texas ferry-man wearing a stiff new Stetson and linen duster over his only suit, an old woman named Newkirk in a sturdy dress and one of those cinderproof tie-down hats who claimed a daughter and son-in-law in Fort Sumner, and me—jounced and swayed and caromed off the mud wagon's ironwood frame all the way from El Paso to the City of Widows, sickening of the pervasive dust, one another, and above all our own company before we'd gone ten miles. When the fer-ryman learned Mrs. Newkirk was bound for the place where Billy the Kid was slain, he honored us with his firsthand account of the time the Kid stuck up a bank that was holding the mortgage of a destitute widow, gave the money to the widow so she could settle the mortgage, then stuck up the same banker again as he was leaving the widow's house with the money. The Bonney legend seemed to be taking a new turn, from efficient killer to crafty saint. If I hung around long enough I'd hear of him changing the Alamosa River to wine.

Approaching San Sábado, the coach slowed for a bootjack and I spotted a familiar lumpy figure on hands and knees atop the unfinished roof of a frame building that hadn't existed when I left. I shouted to

the driver to stop, hopped out without a word of fare-
well to my fellow passengers, and hobbled on pins
and needles to the back to untie the claybank. The
shotgun messenger threw down my saddle, bedroll,
and Winchester, the driver snapped the reins, and the
whole improbable waste of good firewood rattled off
towing a plume of New Mexico topsoil. I hadn't been
so glad to see the back of anything since the muster-
ing-out camp in Maryland.

Rosario Ortiz, trapped out in his customary work
kit of overalls, cavalry coat, and stained sombrero, sat
back on his heels on the rooftree and spat a mouthful
of nails into the palm of his hand.

"*Buenas tardes, Señor* Murdock! Shake the hand of
my worthless eldest son Arturo, whom I despair of
ever teaching a trade."

I accepted the strong grip of a black-haired youth
of around sixteen who had been engaged in passing
planks up to his father. Gaunt where the other was
fleshy and more guarded in the face, Arturo nonetheless possessed the Ortiz eyes—large, dark, and all-
absorbent—and the tonsorial bowl of a big family
with plenty of hair to cut and not much time to observe the current modes from the East. I saw too a
potent strain of rebellion, barely masked by the per-
functory politeness. I wondered if he was one of the
pair who had burned down the schoolhouse.

"Not another saloon, I hope," I said to the marshal.

"Better than that, *señor*. Colonel Ripperton's harness shop has outgrown the second floor of the livery
and he has secured a loan from the bank in Socorro
City to build and stock a new store on this spot, where

the cattle companies will see it first thing as they enter town. There will be rooms to let upstairs and space in back where the ladies may purchase hats and gingham. This is progress, yes?"

"I hope he plans on stocking plenty of black."

"A merchant can starve serving the widows. He is preparing for the ladies to come. Everyone is talking about the sheriff's investment in the Apache Princess. It is said that he can smell gold. There is talk of a hotel and a theater, and perhaps even the railroad will come to San Sábado someday. If all this comes to pass I shall have to hire an assistant. Arturo is less than no help at all, and his brothers and sisters are worse." He removed his sombrero and mopped his coatsleeve across his forehead. It must have been hot enough to fry bacon up on that roof.

"Anything new in town?"

"I do not know. I have not been there in five days." He pointed at a bedroll spread out on the floor of the half-finished building. "I think no one has been shot, or someone would have come out and told me."

"Ortiz, how did you ever come to be marshal?"

He clamped the nails between his teeth and spoke around them as he lined one up between thumb and forefinger at the end of a joist. "The old padre, he says, 'Rosario, you have served in the Army of Mexico, you can shoot a gun, yes?' I say yes, but it has been a long time. 'Rosario, at night the coyotes come down from the hills. They dig in the church garden looking for moles, drop their waste in the cemetery, and get in fights outside the door during Mass. I appoint you marshal so that you may shoot them. The city will pay you five silver dollars at the end of each

week for keeping the peace and ten cents for each
coyote you shoot inside San Sábado.' The carpentry
business, it is not so good at this time I am speaking of.
I say yes. This was five years ago. Now the old padre is
in the cemetery and the coyotes no longer come
down from the hills, but I still go to the back door of
the church at the end of each week and there the new
padre hands me a sack containing five dollars and
counts the dead rats I have brought and gives me a
dime for each one. The coyotes ate the rats, you see."
He pounded the nail home with his hammer.

"Can you come down from that roof? My neck is
stiff enough from the ride without having to look up
at you while I talk."

"*Lo siento*, I cannot. I have but two hours of daylight in which to work. The colonel wants to move in
Sunday."

"He'll have to wait. I've got marshaling business
that has nothing to do with rats or coyotes."

He sighed a Mexican sigh, full of revolutions and
piety, and climbed down the ladder. On the ground
he picked up an Arbuckle's sack and expectorated the
nails into it, then handed it and the hammer to Arturo. He stood in front of me, waiting, with his feet
splayed and his hands open at his sides. I tried to picture him as a soldier but couldn't. Well, the Army of
the Potomac had succeeded in spite of the excess bag-
gage in its ranks.

"I'm just back from old Mexico and the Diamond
Horn Ranch," I said. "Don Segundo has agreed to
provide men for the posse and will meet us in Las
Cruces on the twenty-second."

"Why do you pursue this, *señor?*" He sounded like

the despairing father. "This thing that happened at the saloon, out here it is like a flood or a high wind, a thing that no one can predict or control. You cannot chase the wind."

"I spent six years chasing it up in Montana. Your problem is you think because you can put on and take off that star the job's the same way. You don't stop just because the coyotes have returned to the hills. You have to follow them there and finish them off. Otherwise they'll just come back, and then they won't stop at digging up the garden and disrupting services."

"I think you forget you are in business with Ross Baronet's brother. What will happen to our new prosperity when he learns what you are about?"

"Which do you represent, the law or the chamber of commerce? You agreed to head up a posse once I had Guerrero's support."

He folded his arms across his chest. It was a large expanse and they barely reached.

"I have given my word. I require truth in return. It is a small enough request when a man of my family responsibilities offers his life. What is your difference with the Baronets? I reject the robbery attempt."

I nodded. I'd been expecting something of the sort. "That's fair. Two years ago in Lincoln County, Ross gunned down a rancher named Spooner and his wife. Spooner's father saved the life of the man I work for at the time of the war with Mexico. The man I work for believes Frank was involved in the shooting, either as a participant or as the man who planned it. He wants to try them both in Helena and see them hang."

For a long time the Mexican said nothing. Then he unfolded his arms.

"This I understand. I know of Judge Blackthorne, and of his character, since long before he was Judge Blackthorne. You should have told me this at the beginning." He rummaged inside his pocket and hung the battered star on the front of his coat.

"What have you to offer besides that hunk of tin and your old cap-and-ball?" I asked.

"I shall go to see John Whiteside, with whom I am friendly. He too has reasons to see the soles of the feet of both Baronets. He and Don Segundo have been stealing each other's cattle for fifteen years, but I think this is a business in which they can set aside their quarrel. He will match the don in men and horses and guns."

"You'd better get started. We have less than a week."

He barked at Arturo, who picked up his father's toolbox in both hands. It was three feet long, made of solid maple, and filled to the handle with iron implements. Ortiz stepped up onto the floor of the building and bent to roll up his bedding. I joined him, curious about something he'd said.

"Where do you know Blackthorne from since before he became a judge?"

"I too fought in the war you mentioned, *señor*. I was a prisoner for a time. He was among the *norteamericanos* who held me."

A light dawned. "Cerro Gordo?"

"*Sí*, that is the place where I was captured." He tied the bedroll.

"He told me about a young Mexican lieutenant

who killed three of his guards and escaped to resume fighting the next day. He said the man's name was Ortiz. I didn't think it could be you."

"We grow old and fat, *Señor* Murdock. We change. But on the outside only. The eagle does not die a swallow."

*Of course,* I thought. *And I am President Garfield.*

I rode the claybank into town, turned it over to the Yaquí at the livery for a rubdown and feeding, and carried my gear over to the Apache Princess and my room upstairs. I looked at the bed, wanting it down to my toes, but when you reach forty it's a sound idea to lubricate the aching joints if you expect them to work properly the next day. I went downstairs for a shot, but I never got it. Colleen Bower got up from her table when I entered and intercepted me on the way to the bar. The cowboy she'd been playing with scowled at me and counted his chips.

"Where have you been?" she asked. "I thought you'd gone back to Helena."

"I went south for *Señora* Guerrero's tortillas and a talk with Geronimo. You look like you're rigged for church." It was a sober dress for her, dark blue and buttoned at the throat. Her black hair was tied back and there were tiny fissures at the corners of her eyes where she'd missed with the powder.

"I expected you back before this. Junior's gone. I think he went to Socorro City to kill the sheriff."

I didn't credit it. "Why would he want to do a thing like that?"

"Right after you left he started drinking. It made him sick, but he'd go out back and throw it up and come back in and order another. I told Irish Andy to cut him off. Look what he did to him."

The bald German was polishing the bar, holding his head at an awkward angle to watch his progress. One eye was swollen almost shut and gone rainbow-colored.

"He's lucky. Junior's been known to break jaws when he's on a tear. That little frame of his fools you."

"He got it in his head somehow the sheriff had come between you. If he weren't around you'd forget about upholding the law and take care of business here. It didn't make sense so I didn't pay much attention."

"That's when you have to pay attention to him most. But you couldn't know that. When did he leave?"

"Yesterday early. I wasn't up yet but the stable hand at the livery said he hired a buckskin. He had on a duster and he was carrying a Spencer rifle."

"I know the one." I'd traded it to him in '72 for a bay mare that splintered its right foreleg in a prairie dog hole the following spring.

"Where are you going?"

"To find Ortiz." This from the door.

"What good is a carpenter going to do you in this situation? Page?"

He was at the mercantile, shoveling food tins from the counter into a canvas sack while the clerk, a schoolmaster by trade and a dish-chested consumptive forced into commerce in the absence of a house of learning, totaled up the order in his ledger.

"I'm glad I caught you," I said to the marshal.

"There was no need for haste, *señor*. I cannot leave before morning. The days grow short."

"There's been a change in plans. I won't be meeting you and Don Segundo's men in Las Cruces. I'll be waiting for you in Socorro City." I told him about Junior.

He frowned, the ends of his tobacco-stained moustaches nearly meeting. "Frank Baronet is not a man to call out. It is more than just his badge that makes him sheriff. I hope that you and your friend did not exchange cross words before you parted. Surely he is dead. All that remains is for him to fall down."

"You haven't seen him use that Spencer. He's a good man with a rifle."

"Jubilo is better, and he is always within rifle range of his friend Baronet." He paid for his purchases—in silver dollars—and gathered up the sack. "You have not told me where I should look for you in Socorro City."

"I'll find you. It shouldn't be so hard with all that firepower you'll have along, with or without John Whiteside. When you see him, tell him he did a fine job with the claybank."

"I will do this."

I went back to the Princess, truly too tired now to sit up and drink. Instead I climbed the stairs to my room with no thought beyond sleep; concern for Junior, with dusk rolling in and my bones turning to lead, would serve neither of us. I felt as if I'd walked all the way from El Paso.

Someone knocked while I was climbing into bed. I

pulled on my trousers, hooked the Deane-Adams out of its holster hanging on the bedpost, and took aim at the door from the far corner. "Who is it?"

"Colleen."

I took the revolver off cock and went over and opened the door. She was dressed as she had been earlier, but either she had done something about her makeup or the failing light canting in through the window had decided to be kind to her. She looked little more than school age.

"There's gray in your hair but not on your chest," was the first thing she said. "I've wondered about that."

"I use my brain a lot more than my heart. Is anything wrong?"

"No. Yes."

I closed the door behind her, returned the gun to its holster, and set fire to the lantern. Orange light spread.

"I didn't tell you everything today," she said. "Junior proposed to me."

"I'll be damned."

"It happened in the saloon the day you left. He caught me off guard. I didn't realize he felt anything toward me more than one partner to another."

"I'll be damned."

"He was drunk at the time. I didn't think he was serious. I laughed. I told him I was already married."

"Did you tell him who?"

"Yes." She licked her lips; something I had never seen her do. "That's when he started talking about killing Frank Baronet."

*I'll be damned.*

# ⤙ 18 ⤚

"FRANK BARONET." IT was as if I had never heard or said the name before. Like Billy the Kid he was something I had not known existed until recently and already he was filling my life.

She said nothing. There was murk in the blue depths of her eyes, as if something had stirred near the bottom, churning up silt. Just what it was, I had no hopes of ever understanding.

I felt my head nodding. I had the impression it had been doing so for some time. "I don't know why I didn't guess. When I met you, you were the mistress of a dead city marshal. Then you started keeping company with me. You always did feather your nest by latching on to the local law."

"You were different," she said. "I'll never make you believe it but it's true. I don't apologize for the others. You don't know what it's like for a woman on the circuit. When you fall into a fix you can fight your way out of it and if the odds don't favor fighting you can jump into the saddle and ride hard. I cannot fight, and I cannot jump in these petticoats. I've been beaten and jailed and raped. That can happen to you only so many times before you realize you need the same edge in life you look for in cards."

"What became of your edge in El Paso?"

"There is too much law there and it is all split up." She changed the subject. "In Socorro City, where I set up last year, you either dealt faro at the Orient or you cut Frank Baronet in for fifty percent. I chose the Orient. It turned into something."

"It generally does, although not always marriage. How did that come about?"

"You wouldn't notice, but Frank is an attractive man, and wealthy. Jim Dolan has his eye on him for governor when statehood comes."

"Do you believe that?"

"I did then. I do now. That old fool Fremont did less for Garfield than Frank did for Dolan before Lew Wallace came, and now Fremont is territorial governor in Arizona. I was in a tight, Page. The Civic Betterment League ran me out of Leadville with nothing but the clothes on my back and a pearl necklace that got me as far as Santa Fe. I picked a pocket there and took another train. The pocket belonged to a Dolan man who wired my description to Frank. He was waiting for me when I got off in Socorro."

"Is that when he proposed?"

She was silent for a moment.

"I cannot talk to you," she said then. "I could in Breen. You've changed."

When she started to turn away I grasped her arm

and pulled her into the room. She tried to pull free. I took her other arm and held on. The material of her dress touched my naked chest.

"So it was jail or a table at the Orient," I said. "Baronet is not a man to overlook a good draw. And he favors a corner, so he dangled a wedding ring. You liked his chances, and marriage to the biggest gun in the county comes in handy when those cowboys and miners forget what side of the table they're supposed to sit on. Then Wallace settled the war up north and Baronet's chances didn't look so good, so you left. You never were one to hang around when the glitter wore off a thing."

She tried to knee me in the crotch. I let go of her to make distance. She backed up a step, but she didn't leave. Instead she raised her hands to her head and spread her hair to the left of the part. There was another part there, jagged and white and freshly healed. It would be a long time before hair grew along it, if it ever did. She said:

"I don't even remember what the argument was about. He slapped me around, not for the first time, and then he drew that big rolling-block pistol and backhanded it. If I hadn't turned my head it would have split my face open from forehead to chin. He tried again, but I got hold of my bag and the pocket Remington. At first he was surprised. Then he laughed, called me a whore, and turned his back on me. His *back.* I shot him. He fell on his face. I guess I should have made sure he was dead, but I had blood in my eyes. I was afraid he'd cracked my skull.

"It happened in my room over the Orient," she went on. "It was Saturday night, the place was noisy.

No one heard the shot. I went down the back stairs and bled all the way to the doctor's office, where I got my scalp sewn back together. I said I fell. Doc Sullivan was no idiot—he'd patched me up before after Frank and I had words—but he didn't say anything. He gave me something to make me sleep, but I poured it out when he wasn't looking. His wife gave me some old clothes to wear back to my room and they left me alone to change. I let myself out the window. I never stole a horse before, but I was sure I'd be hunted for a murderess. I caught up with the train in San Marcial and rode it to El Paso."

"He told me he hurt his back when a horse threw him."

"Would you expect him to say a woman shot him?"

"Why did you come back to New Mexico?"

"By the time Junior Harper came to town to buy fixtures for the Princess, I'd heard Frank had recovered, which meant I wasn't wanted since he'd never admit what happened. 'Unknown assailant,' the wire reports said. My run was going sour and I had just enough capital left to take Junior up on his offer to buy in. You could argue that I was just swimming back into the same net, but it was a net I knew. You don't always have choices. You almost never have choices."

"You didn't put up an argument when I suggested cutting the sheriff in on the Princess."

"His money spends just like anyone else's. And I was curious to know if getting shot by me had changed his outlook."

"Risky."

She moved a shoulder. "That's why they call it gambling."

"Not when you throw someone like Junior into the pot. Then it's called something else."

"We both did that, Page."

I said nothing, agreeing.

She turned her head slightly, reading me like a deck. "You love him, don't you?"

"We go back."

"Maybe he'll turn around when he sobers up."

"He never has."

"What are you going to do when you get to Socorro City?"

"What I should have done the first day I saw the place." I had turned and was thumbing cartridges out of a Union Metallic box into the empty loops on my gun belt. "Vote the sheriff out of office."

# ↳◦ 19 ◦↴

FOR A MILE under the creeping crimson in the east, my route and Marshal Ortiz's were the same, and we rode together. He sat a well-fed gray with a brand I didn't recognize and his sack of provisions knotted unceremoniously to the horn of a Mexican cavalry saddle. The saddle's fenders had been trimmed and pared many times for leather to make repairs. A brass-framed Henry rifle hung from the ring.

If we hadn't been the only things stirring in town when we encountered each other in front of the livery, I wouldn't have known him. He'd traded his overalls for faded cavalry breeches with a stripe up the side and a knitted blue pullover of a type I hadn't seen since my last skirmish with the guerrillas in Missouri. The greasy somberero was gone, replaced by a slouch hat with all the nap worn off the brim in front where he gripped it to tug it down over his eyes, and on top of the cavalry coat he wore crossed bandoliers

crammed with .44 cartridges with only their blunt
lead noses showing so as not to catch the sun on the
brass. The curved butt of a Schofield .44 fitted with
black walnut grips showed above a plain holster worn
in front like an Elizabethan codpiece. With his high-
topped riding boots sporting long jingly Mexican
spurs, he looked taller and fitter in the outfit than he
had at any time previously, and more a part of the
land; one with the snakes and scorpions and lean
rangy beasts of prey that slunk among the shadows
carved by the rocks in the desert.

"That rig hasn't been sitting in any trunk since
Cerro Gordo," I said by way of greeting.

"I scouted for Colonel MacKenzie in 1874." He
handed the sleepy stable boy a coin and took charge
of the gray.

"You fought Quanah Parker?"

"He was just Quanah then. Parker came with the
reservation."

I had been riding the line at the Harper Ranch
with Junior when the news came of Ranald MacKenzie's defeat of the Comanche Nation in Palo Duro
Canyon in 1874. It had brought a sudden end to more
than thirty years of fighting in Texas. Nearly everyone
involved in the engagement had been decorated for
valor. On the road he made a coarse noise when I
asked him about the battle.

"It was a slaughter of horses. I do not talk about
it."

Where the road forked we drew rein. I told him
again I'd see him near Socorro City and offered my
hand. He hesitated, then took it.

"I hope *Señor* Harper is all right."

"Me too."

Once we parted I began paying special attention to the irregularities in the landscape, rock piles and buttes and thickets that held so much appeal for hostiles who didn't wish to be observed. By midday, however, the absence of Apaches had begun to become obvious, and when eight hours later I made camp I felt certain I was alone. Well, Geronimo and his band had been headed somewhere when Axtaca and the vaqueros and I encountered them below the border, and there were rumors that the Apaches were concentrating on Arizona. That placed them in General Crook's wheelhouse, which was good enough for me. There was a strong case to be made in favor of all the tribes but that one. If they were alone on the planet they'd have picked a fight with the moon.

On the ridge overlooking the county seat I paused to gaze down at the teeming sprawl at my feet. Hammering and sawing, the heartbeat and respiration of civilization birthing in the wilderness. While it was going on, life glowed. When it stopped, decay set in. Only sometimes the rot was present in the fresh lumber, growing unheeded during the construction, spreading to the healthy timbers and eating away at the joints and pegs, so that six months or even six weeks later the entire structure collapsed, taking lives with it. Often that rot was human. Sometimes it wore a badge.

I conferred with my dented pocket watch, the posthumous gift of a Confederate captain. Unless Frank Baronet had altered his routine, he would be dealing faro at the Orient about now, leaving Jubilo

No-Last-Name in charge of the jail. It seemed a likely place to start.

The gate leading inside the board fence that enclosed the gallows and surrounding courtyard was latched as simply as possible, with a piece of lath secured by a nail. I'd been counting on that, breaking into jail not being as popular a practice as breaking out. On the other side, the scaffold threw a shadow that clasped the back of my neck like a clammy hand. The back door to the building was solid oak, set flush to the frame, and probably bolted and padlocked inside, but that wasn't how I was planning to get in so I ignored it. The single barred window on that side of the building, designed to allow light into the cells rather than to let the residents see outside, was nearly seven feet from the ground. I grasped the brick sill in both hands and chinned myself up.

No lamps burned inside and the sun was coming in at a flat angle. In the murky light I couldn't tell if any of the cots in the cells were occupied. I tried tapping on the thick glass.

"You won't find him in there."

I didn't turn my head at the sound of the voice behind me. I let go of the sill and spun when I landed, gripping the butt of the Deane-Adams.

I didn't take it out. The tunnel I was looking down belonged to Jubilo's Creedmoor. Its owner was standing at the other end with the butt against his shoulder and his finger on the trigger. The gallows rose gaunt and empty at his back.

"Well, toss it over."

I slid the five-shot out of its holster between

thumb and forefinger and gave it a low flip so that it landed gently at his feet. He lowered the rifle but kept it balanced along his forearm as he crouched to pick up the revolver. He found the catch and thumbed the cylinder around, tipping the cartridges out onto the ground. His eyes remained on me. They were almond-shaped after his Indian ancestors. The face under the flat brim of the Stetson, with darts of black whisker at the corners of the wide mouth, was unreadable. He handled the long-barreled rifle in one hand as easily as a sidearm. So far I had never seen him make use of the Russian on his hip, and I decided it was an ornament of office.

"Always keep a live round under the hammer?" he asked.

"Empty chambers attract drafts. I catch cold easy."

"Shoot your dick off someday."

"That's what everyone says. But it's still there and I'm still here."

He tossed it back. I caught it. "I guess you know where the gate is."

The rifle was resting on his shoulder now. I blew dust out of the pistol's action, returned it to its holster, and preceded him into the alley. Behind me he paused to set the latch on the gate.

On the street we walked side by side to the end of the block. He carried the rifle with the muzzle angled down. He stopped in front of a new brick building, opened the door, and held it. The lettering on the plate glass show window read:

P. JOHNS & SON
UNDERTAKERS

It was a dark, heavy room, thickly carpeted and swaddled in wine-colored velvet and black oak. A mahogany casket with brass handles lay open on a padded dais with a bald-headed geezer propped up inside wearing a morning coat and a stiff collar. Another one, nearly as old and dressed similarly but more lively looking, with a rubber face and small bright eyes like shirt studs, bustled out of a back room at the sound of the entry bell, buttoning his vest. Jubilo pointed at the curtains the man had just come through and kept walking. I accompanied him.

The back room was nearly as large as the parlor but made no pretense at ornamentation. Large windows set near the ceiling allowed sunlight to pour in onto a bare plank floor strewn with packing material, a long oilcloth-covered workbench at the back, and sawhorses. Two of the sawhorses supported a plain pine box without a lid. The air was thick with ammonia and formaldehyde.

Jubilo hung behind while I stepped forward and looked down inside the box. The undertaker had done little more than wash his face. There was dust in the creases of his Prince Albert and fancy vest—he hadn't bothered to change clothes for the long ride—and a couple of stitches had been taken in the hole in the silk where the bullet had either gone in or come out, but nothing had been done about the bigger hole in his left sock where two of his long sharp-nailed toes stuck through. His dark hair was plastered back with water, accentuating the narrowness of his skull, the caverns in his cheeks, the long treadle jaw and the bulbous eyes, barely closed, resting like billiard balls in their sockets. Those eyes had never warmed the air with their moist glow. That face had never slid off-kilter to illuminate a room with its crooked grin. His skin had the gray translucence of paraffin.

"Two questions." My own voice sounded hollow, like someone else speaking in a room at the end of the house.

"Me," Jubilo said. "He was standing in the street in front of the Orient, waving a Spencer and calling the sheriff every kind of a son of a bitch. That made him a public menace. I shot him from a window on the second floor of the Chicago House. I couldn't wait for him to turn around. I guess that's the second question."

"Did Baronet even get up from his table?"

"Hell, he wasn't even in town. He's off collecting taxes. I hated to do it, if it means anything. I liked the little guy right off when we met in San Sábado. He didn't make no secret what he thought of Frank even when he was asking him for a loan."

I turned to face him. "How far out is Baronet's ranch?"

After a pause he showed his eyeteeth.

"Well, all he told me was to say he's out collecting taxes. He didn't say nothing about anyone guessing. Head straight east for a day. Keep Chupader Mesa square in front and you can't miss it. It's a thousand acres. I won't ask who told you about it."

"The White Lion of Chihuahua."

His face didn't change. "You do get around," he said. "Might could be there is something to this Satan's Sixgun business after all."

"What happens now? Am I under arrest?"

"What for, trespassing on public property? Go back to the Widow City, Murdock. Socorro County will bury your friend."

"Tell the undertaker to put him in the icehouse. I'll be back for him."

"Don't go after him, amigo."

His tone made me turn back. "How many guns does Ross have?"

"Ross is dead."

"That train pulled out a long time ago, Jubilo."

"Habit." He moved his shoulders. "A dozen. More, maybe. They drift in and out. Not all as good as those two you killed in San Sábado, but good enough to side the Baronets is good enough for anyone, and they know the ground. But they are not Ross's guns. They answer to Frank. Always did. Ross never pulled up his britches but that Frank gave him leave."

"Don't read over me just yet. I should have been dead twenty years ago and a hundred times since. Others keep taking my place."

"I just hope it isn't me kills you," he said. "It wouldn't be the first time I done it to someone I liked. I can do without what comes after."

"Did you like the Spooners?"

Light dawned. Absently, he nodded. "That's what this is about. I wondered. What was Dave Spooner to you?"

"To me, nothing." I told him about Judge Blackthorne, Sergeant Uriah Spooner, and the siege of Monterrey. He nodded again.

"I was there when Dave and Vespa got it," he said. "I didn't pull the trigger. Ross done that. It was Frank sent us out there. A lot of Chisum's men looked up to Dave. Frank thought if we killed both of them the rest would see Dolan meant business."

"Did they?"

"It never works that way. Dolan got mad as hell. He didn't order it or know about it until it was over and done with. He said if there was ever a chance of Wallace not bringing in the army and spoiling everything, that chance went into the ground with Dave and Vespa Spooner."

"You're telling me when you and Frank and Ross left Lincoln, it wasn't the army you were running from."

"You can always avoid an army. I don't think Jimmy Dolan shot a gun in his life, but if he ever come close to using one on anybody, it would of been Frank. I think the whole reason he got Frank elected sheriff here was to keep him out of Lincoln. I think he thought if he didn't and Frank came back, Dolan would of killed him sure as hell."

"Frank's living on borrowed time," I said.

"Not borrowed. Stole."

"What keeps you with him?"

"What keeps you with the Judge?"

"It's different."

"For you, maybe. Not me. When you're half greaser and half Comanche and you know one end of a rifle from the other, backing someone like Frank Baronet is as high as you can reach. It's one hell of a lot higher than if you didn't have the rifle."

"Where were you when Colleen shot him?"

"I don't follow him into bedrooms," he said. "She told you, I guess. In that case you can take her a message from Frank. Tell her he don't hold what she done against her. He wants her back."

"So he can finish beating her up?"

He blinked. "Did she tell you he done that? Frank never done that."

"Just in bedrooms, I guess."

"I've known Frank right around five years. Rode with him, camped with him, stood up with him when he hitched up with Colleen. He'd maybe kill a woman, but he never beat one up. Should of, some of the ones he run with. He never did. It's a failing."

"She showed me the scar."

"Her head, right?"

I said nothing.

"A Mexican whore done that. They called her Juanita Pistola on account of this old pepperbox she carried around to scare folks with. It wouldn't shoot. She tried splitting open Colleen's head with the barrel when she found out about the wedding. Frank shot her."

"Then why did Colleen shoot Frank?"

"Like I said, I don't follow him into bedrooms."

I exhaled. All my energy went out with the bad air. I felt bone weary.

"Ride south, Jubilo," I said. "Don't stop before old Mexico. There's an army coming you can't avoid."

"I figured out that much when you mentioned Don Segundo. I reckon I'll stick. I got more enemies down there than I do here, and there's nothing waiting for me up north but a rope. What the hell, I never was no good at making a choice anyway. Just where are you riding with this here army?"

I dug the nickel-plated star engraved DEPUTY U.S.

MARSHAL out of my trouser pocket and pinned it to my shirt. Once again he nodded.

"Out front. I guessed that too," he said. "By the by, a wire come in this morning from Santa Fe. Garfield died last week."

"Sorry to hear it. I voted for him." I waited.

"Point is, if the office of president don't turn away bullets, how much protection do you think you'll get from that tin plate?"

## ᔟᔚ **20** ᔟᔚ

THE RIFLE REPORT rang thin and insignificant in the vast night air. I caught the fading phosphorescence of the muzzle flash in a clump of cottonwoods to the north and stood in my stirrups, waving my Winchester over my head. A three-quarter moon washed the open plain in watery silver.

"I'll need a name," called a voice.

"Page Murdock. Ortiz knows me."

"Step down and come ahead. Keep your hands in sight."

He was small and young and well turned out for his work in a pinch hat, leather vest and chaps, and those torturous boots with pointed toes that bowed their legs and made them hobble around when not in the saddle. His rifle was an old Volcanic with scroll-work on the receiver and someone's initials carved into the stock in big childish capitals.

"Your father's?" I pointed at the rifle.

His lips were tight behind his puppy moustache. "Walk ahead."

The campfire smelled inviting after a week of cold prairie nights without a fire lest I attract the attention of Jubilo or one of Baronet's bandits. I had seen the dust of a large band of horses shortly before sundown and cut a course for the glow of the fire after dark.

"I figure you're with Whiteside," I said, walking. "You don't look like one of Don Segundo's vaqueros."

He grunted.

"Bad enough I got to ride with them without getting took for one."

I spotted Ortiz first, squatting by the campfire with a stick in his hand, drawing designs in the dirt between him and John Whiteside, also squatting on his heels. The marshal had on his slouch hat and cavalry clothes but had removed the bandoliers. The old rancher, built even slighter than his lookout but lean as a salt rind, wore his big sombrero and a sheepskin coat with the left sleeve hanging empty. His whiskers looked grayer in the firelight. Both men were intent on what the Mexican was doing with the stick.

"Chupader," Whiteside muttered. "I seen easier places to defend but not lately. I and forty men fit eleven Apaches there for a week back in '68. All it takes is one good man with a rifle."

"They've got that."

Both men turned their heads my way. Whiteside's blue eyes scarcely lingered on the badge I wore. "Took on weight, I see."

The young cowboy said, "He come riding up bold

as Maggie's nipples, Colonel. Asked for the greaser marshal."

"I know him. Get back to your watch. Abbott," he said when the man started to turn.

"Yes, Colonel?"

"You might want to hold off on that greaser talk till we get back home. Half the men you're riding with are greasers and they might not all be as accommodating as Marshal Ortiz."

"I don't know why we're riding with them a-tall. I guess the men of the Slash W can handle one slippery sheriff without dragging along a bunch of pepperguts."

"You were still on the tit the first time I crossed lead with pepperguts from the Diamond Horn. They put better men than you in the ground. If it was a case of one slippery sheriff I'd of done the job alone. Once you've put your first ball through something that can defend itself better than a colicky prairie hen, you can bellyache all you want. Till then, get back to your watch."

"Yes, Colonel." He left.

"Pup."

"He is young." Ortiz rose, dropping the stick, and pulled his sleeve down over his hand to scoop a two-gallon coffeepot off a flat rock by the fire. "When was the last time you thought you could fight bad *hombres* all the day and make love to bad *mujeres* until the dawn?"

"Cold Harbor. And if I'd had this new batch with me then there would still be slaves in Carolina. Pull up a piece of ground, Murdock. How you getting on with that claybank I sold you?"

"I haven't eaten him yet. He's tied up back there. I fed and watered him before I broke camp."

"I gelded that one myself. Hated to do it, but there was no help for it. Stallions have a way of catching some Apache filly's scent and blowing just when you're looking for quiet. I was pleased to see he kept his spirit."

The marshal handed me the tin cup he'd filled from the pot. He searched my face. "Have you seen *Señor* Harper?"

"I saw him. He didn't see me." I took the cup in both hands, warming them, and poured the hot bitter stuff down my throat. It brought a glow to my stomach like good whiskey.

"*Lo siento.* He was a good man."

"He was a jackass. I don't know how he lived as long as he did."

Brushing past me on the way back to his spot by the fire, he laid a hand on my shoulder briefly.

"You said they have a good man with a rifle," Whiteside said. "That would be Jubilo."

"I saw him snatch an Apache brave off his pony's back at four hundred yards. If the mesa's as good a perch as you say, he could take his time and pick us all off one by one like ticks."

"Not at night."

Miguel Axtaca had slid from the shadows outside the firelight, making no noise at all in a pair of soft Apache boots designed to pull up over the knees in cactus country; the flaps were secured around his calves with thongs. His square features, less flexible, were unchanged from when I had seen them last in El Paso del Norte on the way back from the Guerrero ranch. As always he appeared to wear no weapon.

"We have a hundred men," Whiteside told him. "You cannot move a party that size in the dark. They would trip over each other."

"One man alone has no one to trip over."

"Only himself. What will you do when you get there? It's a big mesa and you don't know where he will be."

"I will once he starts shooting."

"What then? Do you intend to place a hex upon him with that medicine bag you carry?"

"The bag is for the protection of my soul. For the protection of my body I use this." He reached behind his neck and produced a knife with a nine-inch blade, its handle bound with rawhide.

I said, "That's close work. Are you any good at it?"

"Ask Francisco and Carlos."

"How are you with that rifle?" Whiteside asked Ortiz.

The marshal had picked up his stick and resumed making marks in the earth. "A Henry is not a Creedmoor. Within its range I am adequate."

"Just so you're good enough to shoot this Indian son of a bitch if he cannot do all he claims."

Axtaca returned the knife to its sheath without another word. The animosity between the Aztec and the old campaigner was as thick as the woodsmoke in the air.

"Baronet took over the old Sherman spread," said the rancher. "The headquarters was just a dugout shack last time I was there."

"He has built a fine house with many rooms with good lumber from the Oscuros," Ortiz said.

"How do you know this?"

"I built it."

"Well, now, that's right handy." Whiteside was disgusted.

"I am a carpenter, *señor*. I am the son of a carpenter and if just one of my sons proves to be less worthless than I fear, he, too will be a carpenter. You are a cattleman. *Señor* Murdock is a saloonkeeper. Miguel is a ranch foreman. We are none of us warriors, yet we have all made war and we are all still living. In the light of this I do not see cause to defend what each of us does when he is not fighting."

"Save it for Sunday. What's the layout?"

While we had been talking the marshal had drawn a floor plan in the dirt. Now he used the stick as a pointer. "It is a house a man might conceive whose conscience is troubled. This is a tower room of three stories, open on all sides, from which a man with good eyes may observe a rider approaching from a great distance. The windows on the ground floor have oak shutters two inches thick, with gun ports. All of the roofs are pitched steep, that none who is not part fly can hope to scale them. Of course there is no ground cover within rifle range of the house."

I said, "Is that all?"

"*Lo siento*, no. The basement is eight feet deep, lined with stones and mortar, and has many shelves and cabinets for the storage of provisions. The well is there. With only a small trapdoor to defend, a man in that dark hole might withstand a siege of many months."

Whiteside stared at him. "Didn't any of this make you curious?"

"The sheriff said he wished to secure the house against an Indian attack. I thought it was excessive."

"It shouldn't, but it always surprises me," I said. "The lengths some men will go to in order to stay out of jail."

"Even build one of his own." Axtaca eyed the plan gravely.

"It *is* a jail," Whiteside said. "Ain't it?"

We looked at him. His eyes were as bright as pennies.

Axtaca left camp twenty minutes later. Francisco and Carlos, unchanged from when I had last seen them at the Diamond Horn, wanted to go with him, but he rebuffed them in harsh Spanish, bundled his sorrel's hoofs in rags torn from his only other shirt, and rode off at a walk armed with only his knife and medicine bag. Whiteside had turned in by then, having dispatched a rider to the Slash W on an errand, and the entire encampment was settling in for the night. Men snored, spoke in low rumbling voices of past battles won and lost in and out of town, cleaned and loaded weapons, and scraped mud off their boots in the glow of dying fires. I poured myself a second cup of coffee and drained the pot's remaining contents into Ortiz's.

"Any trouble getting Whiteside to throw in with Guerrero's men?" I sat down beside him.

"Very little. When two men have been fighting as long as they, the thing they share is not so different from love. It was this way with my wife and me." He crossed himself and drank.

"You said you killed her."

"I took no pleasure in it. She pleaded with me to do it. I swore the day we married that I would deny her nothing."

"She asked you to kill her?"

"She said if I did not agree to do this thing she would find a way to do it herself. I could not let her soul go to hell and so I agreed."

"Was she ill?"

"Her body was healthy. In here . . ." He touched his head and shook it.

I said nothing. The wood in the fire separated slowly into coals, and I thought the conversation was ended.

"It was in the church," he said then. "She knelt before the Virgin, and as she was praying I shot her once in the back of the head. She died in a state of grace."

"I'm sorry."

He moved one of his heavy shoulders. "I lost her long before that day. My sorrow is that we cannot be together in the next life. The bullet that spared her from hell has damned me."

"Did you confess to the padre?"

"No. If one is to be forgiven, he must first be repentant. I would do this thing again."

"The rumor around town is you found her with another man."

"That is the story I told at my trial. A jury of twelve men, husbands all, found me innocent of murder. And Serafina's torment is not spoken of in the saloons of San Sábado."

I drank the rest of my coffee in silence. I had ridden through thickets and mountain passes crammed with ice that were easier to penetrate than his tragedy.

At length I threw the wet grounds into the fire. "Earlier tonight you called Miguel Axtaca by his Christian name. Even Francisco and Carlos don't do that. How far do you go back with him? Spare me the peon humility," I said when he started to reply.

"*Sí.*" He raised and lowered his chin. His jowly profile was a blank cutout against the slightly lighter sky. "In truth we did not meet before Las Cruces, five days ago. However, I read his name many times in dispatches in the old days when we were on opposite sides, and I came to feel that I knew him then."

"Opposite sides of what?"

"The revolution against President Juárez. I was a colonel in his army."

"Ortiz, you're a damn liar."

"I do not lie about these things, *señor.*"

"Not about that. I mean before, when you said you weren't a warrior. I'm wondering when you found time to practice carpentry."

"It is not what we do that makes us what we are, but what we feel. I have not known a day since I learned to think for myself when I did not run my palm along the grain of a piece of wood and feel the life that resides there. Death is nothing. What have you done when you have brought nothing to your fellow man?"

"With some men," I said, "there was nothing there to begin with."

"You are wrong, *Señor* Murdock. There is always something. When you destroy a man you take upon yourself the burden of never knowing what it might have been. When you have spent much of your life destroying men, the burden is sufficient to cause your own destruction."

"If you feel that way, why are you here instead of back in town finishing the harness shop?"

He breathed deeply and drank the rest of his coffee, which must have been ice-cold. "You ask that question of the wrong carpenter, *señor.*"

Soon after that we rolled ourselves up in our blankets, and within minutes Ortiz was snoring. What dreams he dreamt I could not fathom.

# 21

THERE IS AN old Zuni legend, nearly as ancient as Creation itself, that maintains that when Father Sun made the world he dumped all the parts he had left over in New Mexico. The story makes sense when you see Chupader Mesa for the first time pouncing straight up out of the planed country east of Socorro City, fluted at its base and blunted at the top like a spent bullet, with the sun, no longer young and red-faced from the effort, hauling itself over the edge. Faced with such momentous physical evidence in support of a pagan belief, it was no wonder the early Spanish missionaries had made so little headway bringing the natives around to a faith in a tale of floods, apples, and shrubbery ablaze.

Rich as it was, I doubt the local Indian canon encompassed anything as strange as the party now approaching that geological non sequitur: one hundred men and change riding together but separated by their dress, loyalty, and philosophy into two distinct bands with a destination in common. Behind them trailed a pack train and, lurching along a good quarter-mile behind that, a small supply wagon new to the expedition since early that morning, its driver a man whose lost face said he had long ago abandoned his ties to life. His name, if it mattered, was Wendigo, and behind his seat rode death in a box measuring three feet by two.

"The sticks are old," Whiteside had explained when the wagon arrived. "They sweat in this heat and nobody but Wendigo will come near them. He lost his wife and two sons to the cholera last year. He don't care if he blows to pieces."

"Don't you have anything more stable?" I'd asked.

"Governor Wallace has placed an embargo on explosives and ammunition in quantity until the dust settles in Lincoln County. I tried old Mexico, but the lid is even tighter there on account of the revolution, I forget just which one. I have had to give up my mining aspirations for a spell. Not that them two holes in my southwest sixty ever coughed up anything shinier than a salamander."

The vaqueros from Don Segundo's Diamond Horn were a disciplined-looking lot, riding mustangs by and large with both hands on the reins, elbows out, backs as straight as the Springfield carbines and El Tigre Winchesters slung behind their shoulders. Their flat-brimmed hats were secured with strings ending in tassels and worn at an identical angle. It was clear that the White Lion of Chihuahua had not laid aside his military sensibilities when he had turned from

fighting men to raising cattle. John Whiteside's cow-
hands looked almost slovenly by comparison, but
they were armed as heavily and rode like men who
did everything but defecate in the saddle. The one-
armed rancher who led them wrapped the reins of his
big black around his wrist and manipulated the horse
with his knees.

There had been incidents. Breaking camp, a
vaquero and a cowboy had disagreed over the ownership of a canteen, a knife had been produced, and a
Mexican arm splintered when two other cowboys in-
tervened; and in an epilogue, Francisco, who had apparently been placed in charge of Guerrero discipline
in Miguel Axtaca's absence, slashed his quirt across
the face of a Whiteside man on his way to reopen the
argument with pistol drawn, laying the flesh open to
the bone. The marshal of San Sábado, mounted also,
broke up both fights by inserting his gray between the
combatants, one hand resting on the butt of his Schofield. I remembered the stern father frightening a
roomful of unruly children into paralysis by his presence alone on the day we met. It seemed that with
each mile he progressed from his sleepy life in town,
he lost another layer of Rosario Ortiz the fat part-time
peace officer, paring down closer to the young Mexican Army lieutenant who had impressed Harlan
Blackthorne so many years before.

Abbott fell first.

The callow cowhand who had challenged me at
the edge of camp the night before was riding a few
yards to my left and a little in front when he grunted
and slid sideways out of his saddle. He grasped at the
horn, but his fingers refused to close. For a second his

left boot snagged in its stirrup. Then his momentum tugged it free and he fell hard on his shoulder and rolled over half onto his back, broken in the middle. All this took place before the report reached us, drawn so thin by distance it bent double. Near the north end of the mesa a scrap of tissuey smoke scudded across the crags.

*"Down!"* Whiteside's roar bounded off that rock wall. Most of us were off our mounts before the echo made it back, our long guns rattling out of their scabbards. I hauled the claybank over onto its side and was pleased to see it stayed put. For all his grousing about how much time he spent stringing fence, the old rancher still took pains to train his horses for combat.

The same wasn't true of the pack animals, whose death wails drifted our way as the wranglers cut their throats to make breastworks of their carcasses.

"It is Palo Duro all over again." Ortiz was down on one knee behind his supine gray with the barrel of his Henry resting across its ribs. "All day and all night we slaughter the horses. When Quanah returns and sees what we have done, it is his sickness at the sight that makes him surrender."

Patting the claybank's flank for courage—the animal's or mine, it didn't matter which—I crawled on my belly over to where Abbott had fallen. After a minute I crawled back. Ortiz read the news on my face.

"His spine, *sí?*" He shrugged at my reaction. "From the way he fell."

"I said Jubilo slept with that Creedmoor."

A spout of dust erupted in front of my horse. It

snorted and stirred, but I reached across to grasp its bit and it subsided. The sound of the shot followed. Somewhere among us a Winchester spoke back.

"Hold your fire, you damn idjit!" Whiteside. "You're just throwing away cartridges."

"I hope that sorrel of Axtaca's didn't put its foot wrong last night," I said.

"I think it did not, *señor*. Even if it did he would continue. He was the only soldier not of rank whose name appeared in the dispatches."

"Oh, Mama, I'm hit!" This from a point somewhere ahead. We heard the shot.

I said, "Right about now I'd settle for something a lot less showy, like a buffalo gun."

Something moved at the top of the mesa then. A human silhouette separated itself from the rock, craning high. More smoke blossomed, a series of ovals pushed in instantly by the wind and torn away. Then: *crack-crack-crack-crack-crack-crack.*

"That was no single-shot Remington," Ortiz said.

"That was a pistol," I said.

"Miguel did not have a pistol."

"Jubilo did."

"What does it mean?"

"One way to find out." I pointed the Deane-Adams at the sky and emptied the cylinder. The shots flopped around in the distance and expired.

In the silence that followed, the man atop the mesa stood up the rest of the way, waving a rifle high over his head. Then he bent. Something fell from the rock. Fell and fell, turning in the air. A man. It struck the ground, bounced, and lay still. Again the man on top stood and waved the rifle.

A hundred feet in front of me, Francisco rose to his feet, tore off his sombrero, and slapped it at the sky. A shrill cry came from his throat, making all the hairs stand out from my body. In another moment the entire party of Mexican vaqueros and American cowboys was cheering.

"I liked Jubilo," I said.

Ortiz said, "If it was not he who killed your friend *Señor* Harper, he had a hand in it."

"He confessed to it. I can't help who I like."

"Frank Baronet has much to answer for."

We buried young Abbott where he fell, scratching a trench in the hard earth with what tools we had and covering him with rocks. Standing over the unmarked mound, John Whiteside removed his sombrero.

"Lord, we give you Jim Abbott, aged about twenty-two years. He pulled his own truck and sent home half his wages first of every month. Dick Lunghammer here says Jim told him his people made him study the piano, but none of us ever heard him play. I guess that's all about Jim."

Wedging the hat under the stump of his left arm, he extracted a small cylinder of oilcloth from inside the sweatband, jerked loose the tie with his teeth, and thumbed through a number of closely printed leaves folded inside. When he found the one he wanted he snapped it open and dropped the rest inside the crown. His harsh ramrod's voice rose as he read.

" 'If he smite him with an instrument of iron, so that he die, he is a murderer. The murderer shall surely be put to death.

" 'And if he smite him with throwing a stone, wherewith he may die, and he die, he is a murderer. The murderer shall surely be put to death.

" 'Or if he smite him with a hand weapon of wood, wherewith he may die, and he die, he is a murderer. The murderer shall surely be put to death.

" 'The revenger of blood himself shall slay the murderer. When he meeteth him, he shall slay him.' Amen." He retrieved the oilcloth, returned it and the pages to the sweatband, and walked away, putting on the sombrero.

I watched Ortiz crossing himself. "I don't think that was your Testament."

"I am a good Christian, *señor*, or I was." He tugged on his slouch hat. "This does not mean I am blinded by my faith. The Holy Book is a gun with two calibers. One will suffice where the other falls short."

We mounted and rode. There were no further squabbles among our party.

The house stood nearly in the shadow of Chupader Mesa, a complicated arrangement of turrets, gables, and railed balconies, whitewashed blindingly in the relentless sun, a sharp contrast to the gray barn standing two hundred yards away with its slanted roof reaching almost to the ground. The sentry post Ortiz had described stretched a full story above the rest of the house and resembled nothing so much as a church tower minus its bell. There would be a rifleman crouching there to avoid silhouetting himself in the opening. There would be others as well, in the windows on the lower floors and in the loft of the barn. The grounds looked far too deserted for a working ranch in broad daylight. The shots from the mesa would have alerted the Baronets and their men long before the lookout had spotted us.

The loft opened up first, jets of flame spurting from the opening over the doors.

"Back!" Again Whiteside's bellow rang. The riders up front wheeled their mounts and galloped. A ragged volley answered from among our ranks, a delaying action while we regrouped. Whiteside passed me aboard his black, drew in, and stood up with the reins in his teeth, beckoning with his arm. The wagon jolted forward from away back.

"He does go forward until he has to back up, doesn't he?" I said to Ortiz.

"It is said that during your War Between the States he reported more casualties for every mile of ground gained than any other commander." The Mexican changed hands on his reins to adjust the bandolier over his left shoulder. "It is also said that he never lost a fight, though he was the only man left on his feet."

"I'm sure he put it just that way in his letters to the widows."

"If he could not lead he would not come. I think you suspected this when you sent me for him."

"I've never been one to stand in the way of a man who likes to ride up front," I said. "That's where the bullets are."

"Nor I, *señor*. And yet no man calls us coward, and you and I count four arms between us."

Whiteside intercepted the wagon and stepped out of leather to supervise the unloading of the dynamite crate. Moments later there was more shouting on his part. I cantered over.

"The fight's that way." I jerked a thumb over my shoulder.

The rancher was red-faced. "You tell him, jackass. I'm still deciding whether to send you home or tie you across a mule and point you toward that barn."

Wendigo, the mule skinner in charge of the wagon, stood with his hat in his hands. He had a beetled brow and black moustaches that folded like crow's wings over the entire lower half of his face. "Some caps got wet crossing the Pecos. You know the railroads won't ship that kind of freight. I had the box marked, but I forgot and taken it instead of one of the others."

"*Blasting* caps, goddamn it!" Whiteside waved one under my nose from the box standing open on the tailgate. It was green with mold and burst at the seam, leaking powder in damp clods. "We got a whole case, and not one of them fit to blow the pus out of a pimple. Dynamite's no good without them. You can set fire to it, Christ, *shoot* at it all day, and all you will get is a ringing in your ears. I wish to hell I could get just one of them to go off. I'd shove it up his ass and send him straight to China."

"There's a way," I said.

After he heard my proposition, Whiteside left me to it and busied himself deploying the men. Francisco translated his orders to the vaqueros. Ortiz, who had donated cartridges to the cause, watched me opening the ends of the sticks with my knife and poking the lead noses inside, leaving the brass primer ends exposed. The shooting from the barn had fallen off.

"You have done this before?"

"Couple of times. Someone is always going off and leaving the caps at home." I laid the finished sticks, dirty green and as long as Christmas candles but twice as big around, on the tailgate and selected a fresh one from the open end of the crate I was sitting on.

"It worked, *sí*?"

"Not even once."

"Mother of God." He crossed himself.

# 22

"BARN OR HOUSE?" I was shoving the finished sticks into a burlap sack.

Ortiz said, "The barn. It is closer to us and commands the best view of the house. The man who takes it has carried the day."

"How is your throwing arm?"

"I have been known to hold my own at horseshoes. How is your marksmanship?"

"Better than my arm." I grasped his when he bent to pick up the sack. "Leave your horse behind. If we clean out the barn, whoever makes for it will have to move fast or get shot out of the saddle by that rifle in the tower. You're too fat."

His face looked tragic. "You are not a politician, *señor*." But he tethered his gray to a low piñon before lifting the sack.

Wendigo, eager to redeem himself for the incident of the blasting caps, climbed into the seat of the wagon and snicked the mules forward to provide cover. Ortiz rode sitting on the tailgate with the sack of dynamite cradled in his lap. I rode the claybank behind, dismounting as we drew within range of the barn and ground-hitching the horse. One of the repeaters in the loft splattered fire. Wendigo, unhitching the team, slapped both mules on the rump and sprinted for cover as they bolted. He didn't seem quite as ready to join his dead wife and children as Whiteside thought.

Ortiz hopped to the ground and together we lifted the back of the wagon and swung it sideways to the barn. A bullet splintered one of the top-bows near the Mexican's head.

"A man could get killed at this work," he said.

"Throw one in front of the doors." I rested the barrel of my Winchester across the seat. "On three."

Crouched on his heels, he selected a stick from the sack, counted, "¡Uno, dos, tres!" and sprang upright, bringing it over his head in a great loop. The stick spun end over end, catching the light on the brass butt of the .44 cartridge stuck in one end. When it landed and stopped rolling I sighted in on the brass. I tugged the trigger.

No explosion.

"Miss?" Ortíz, back in his crouch, stared at me.

"Let's hope." I levered in another shell and fired again.

No explosion.

On the third try I swore I heard the bullet strike metal. The stick spun sideways and rolled to a stop at the base of the barn. I hung my head.

"The fourth time is lucky," Ortiz said. "It was as this when Serafina and I conceived Arturo."

I chambered and fired. The roar lifted the wagon's front wheels an inch off the ground, banging my elbow with the wooden seat. There was white light and a spray of smoke and dust and splinters. One of the big doors swept open and tore loose from its top hinge. It leaned drunkenly for a moment, then the bottom hinge gave and it fell headlong to the ground.

In the great ringing silence that followed, nothing happened. Then the repeater in the loft spoke. The wagon shuddered from the hits.

"Can you put one upstairs?" I asked Ortiz.

"*¡Uno, dos, tres!*"

I followed the stick's cartwheeling motion with the iron sights. Brass glinted just as it entered the square opening. I squeezed. Boards flew and the sky rained shingles. A cheer went up from the men surrounding the house and barn.

"Destroying buildings is much more fun than building them." Ortiz produced another stick. "Shall I throw this one in the same place?"

"Not just yet." There was movement inside the opening to the loft, which was no longer square now, canted left and beribboned with shreds of torn siding. A rifle barrel nosed its way out. I drew a bead.

"Hold your fire!" Whiteside.

I lowered the Winchester. A dirty white rag fluttered from the barrel in the barn.

"Throw it out!" called the rancher. "I have four dozen rifles trained on that hole, so mind what comes out with it."

The rifle emerged out of the shadows inside, attached to a hand and an arm in a pale sleeve. The sleeve was soaked clean through. Streaks of what had soaked it forked down the back of the hand and stained the weapon.

"Colt's revolving rifle," I said.

"Morgan Rood," corrected Ortiz. He was standing now with a fresh stick of dynamite in his hand, watching around the end of the wagon sheet. "I have not seen one in ten years, and with good reason. Perhaps he has shot his own hand."

The rifle dropped then, turning end over end before landing in the dust.

"How many are you?" Whiteside wanted to know.

The answer was barely audible.

"Three. One's in a bad way. I think Hatch is dead."

"Climb down and use the door. We're shooting at anything that moves fast."

This information was greeted with a feeble laugh.

Ortiz made a noise of revelation.

"I know this laughter," he said, when I looked at him. "It is changed, but still I know it."

Five minutes went by that could have passed for as many hours. At length something stirred inside the blasted-open doors at ground level. Another long space of time, and then all was motion.

It had to be one hell of an animal not to have bolted in the face of two explosions. Whatever had held it, it wasn't lack of spirit. The big American stud roan shot through the opening at full gallop, forcing its rider to duck his head to avoid the top of the door frame. In a flash I recognized the corduroy shooting jacket, the black plug hat with a feather in the band, the neat dark beard and big graceful handlebars, the brown jersey gloves with the fingers cut out; details noted in a lump and sorted out later. At the time there was no opportunity to sum them up, because the bloodstained hand that had surrendered the rifle now held a horse pistol and the muzzle was stuttering fire as fast as the hammer could be tipped back and released and tipped back again. He rode straight for the wagon, his mouth gaped in a rebel yell, his torso swiveling to right and left as he sprayed lead in every direction.

I centered my sights on the thickest part of his body, but by the time I fired my first shot, every rifle and carbine in Socorro County was barking. Dust flew off the corduroy jacket in spouts, each hit rocking him in the saddle, and still he came, pumping his trigger finger and directing his fire this way and that. At the end he was so close I heard his hammer snapping on empty shells, for he had spent the cylinder in less time than it took to count the shots. Then the roan threw up its head and turned back upon itself, breaking in half, and horse and rider wheeled over, struck the ground, and slid for several yards, dragging a plume of dust.

Again Whiteside called for a cease-fire.

The roan struggled to rise, snorting and blowing dust out of its nostrils. Its hindquarters, no longer connected to the rest of the animal except by meat and muscle, lay motionless.

"¡Cuidado, señor!" cried Ortiz. But I stepped around the end of the wagon and walked up to where the man lay trapped under his squirming horse. He had lost his hat. Rivulets of sweat had etched tributaries through the skin of dust on his face. He was bleeding in several places. A shard of bone, startlingly white and polished smooth, protruded from a tear below his left elbow. He was supporting himself on his right hand, which still held the empty revolver.

"Are you Ross Baronet?" I asked.

"Kill my horse, mister."

"Are you Ross Baronet?"

"Yes! Please, mister. His back's broken."

"Did you kill Dave and Vespa Spooner?"

"Who?" His face was a mask of pain. Sweat was stinging his eyes. He didn't know me from his raid on the Apache Princess. I was just something between him and the light.

I repeated the names. "In Lincoln County," I prompted.

"Yes."

"What?"

"Yes! I killed them both. Frank said— Please, mister! He's just a poor dumb animal."

"What did Frank say? Did he send you to kill them?"

His arm bent then and he turned his face into the crook of his elbow. He was breathing as heavily as the horse. Sobbing.

I exhaled, placed the muzzle of the Winchester against the hollow behind the roan's left ear, and fired. Its head dropped. Air shuddered out of its lungs.

Cradling the carbine along my forearm, I bent to take hold of Ross under the arms. He was pinned solidly. I straightened to call for assistance. Something thudded against the horse's carcass near the shoulder.

The report, coming from the house, was deep and hoarse. I racked in a cartridge and returned fire, backing up as I worked the lever and trigger. Other rifles rattled from the circle around the house and barn and I sprinted back behind the wagon.

"That was no light repeater," Ortiz said.

"I was wondering what became of Ross's Springfield." I looked at Ross. He was lying as still as the expired roan.

"Dead, probably," said the Mexican, reading my thoughts. "He will remain in that condition this time, I think. I intend to miss him. A man is not responsible for his choice of brothers."

"Forget him. He was a woman-killer." I paused in the midst of reloading to meet his tragic gaze. "Sorry."

He shrugged. *"Está bien.* I shall meet up with him in hell and we shall relive the Battle of Chupader Mesa over tequila."

I finished reloading. "You can shoot at the house all day from this distance without hitting anyone inside. I'm going to try to make it to the loft. Can you reach the porch from here with that dynamite?"

"How close need one come, *señor?* It is dynamite."

"I'll require as much cover as you can lay down. Hitting a moving target with a long-range gun like the Springfield is tricky, and he'll have to reload between shots. Even so, he has the range."

"I have faith in your marksmanship."

It was a curious thing to say. As I was turning his way, he made two long strides, grasped the horn of my saddle, and mounted the claybank. He moved fast for a fat man. For any man. Gathering the reins and thrusting his Henry into the scabbard, he looked down at me. "My arm is tired from throwing, *señor*. It is your turn." And before I could respond he raked his spurs hard. The claybank whinnied and shot forward, grazing my shoulder as it passed the end of the wagon.

I recovered myself in time to send a stream of bullets in the direction of the tower containing the man with the Springfield. The men of the Slash W and the Diamond Horn took my lead and stepped up their fire at the house. Ortiz, hunched low over the claybank's neck, bounded the horse over the corpse and carcass on the ground and galloped directly inside the barn without slowing. A volley came at him from windows on the first and second story of the house, but they were lighter arms than the Springfield and fell short. No shot came from the tower, which was beginning to look as if it had been out in the hail for a year. Pieces of siding hung down like tattered guidons and daylight showed through holes as big as a man's fist.

In less time than I would have thought possible for one of his bulk, Ortiz appeared in the opening to the loft, waving his Henry. Lowering himself to one knee and bracing an elbow against the shattered frame, he snugged the butt of the repeater into his shoulder and waited.

I leaned the Winchester against the wagon, selected a stick from the burlap sack at my feet, made sure the cartridge I'd inserted was secure, drew it back behind my head, and hurled it in the direction of the gingerbread porch, following through with my body. It pinwheeled in a long arc, steeper than I'd intended,

and landed in the short feathergrass ten feet this side
of the wooden steps.

The Mexican showed no disappointment. He took
his time aiming. The Henry coughed. Dust spurted,
the stick jerked and rolled a foot closer to the house.
As soon as it stopped he fired a second time. It went
up, taking a piece of the porch with it. I waited until
debris stopped falling, then threw another. The tra-
jectory this time was flatter and longer. It thumped on
the boards and skidded to a stop against the threshold. When he hit the primer, on his third attempt, the
porch flew apart in a cloud of shattered planks and
amputated pillars. Again the men outside the house
cheered.

The third stick came to rest near the foundation to
the left of the ragged hole where the front door had
been. Ortíz was sighting in on it when a shout came
from inside.

"Don't shoot! We're coming out!"

Some fifty guns posted on that side of the house
leveled on the opening. Inside, the first grasping fingers of flame clambered up the curtain to one of the
windows and scratched at the casing.

One by one, obeying Whiteside's shouted instruc-
tions, seven men stepped down from the ruins of the
porch, weaponless, hands high. Their faces and cloth-
ing were smeared with burnt powder. Two of them
were limping, their trousers slicked with blood. Another two supported a third man between them with
his chin on his chest, half his head apparently blown
away.

There was someone missing, and with Ortiz in

possession of the barn there was only one other place he could be. I checked the load in the Deane-Adams five-shot and contemplated the distance I had to cross to reach the house, burning steadily now and spilling gouts of black smoke out through the bullet-shattered panes.

# 23

I CAST AROUND for the pair of mules Wendigo had un-
hitched from the wagon. Mules are smarter than
horses and rarely stray far from men and the comfort
and security they represent. I spotted them, still
joined by the double harness, grazing in the feathergrass a hundred yards upwind of the noise and
smoke. I found a coil of rope in the wagon and
strolled their way, taking my time to avoid spooking
them. They were skittish, but not nearly as much as
untrained horses would be under those circumstances, and the breeching prevented them from em-
ploying most of their best evasions. I threw the loop
over the head of the near animal, jerked it tight before
it could duck out, and set my heels. After the standard
test of wills, and with strokes and whispered words I
never used with any woman, I got them calm enough
to let me walk them to the wagon.

The cowboys and vaqueros had meanwhile taken

charge of the desperadoes from the house, inspected them for arms, and begun trussing them for transportation to Socorro City or a serviceable cottonwood, whichever was closest. All seemed peaceful, and I was wondering if I weren't being overcautious when the man with the Springfield opened fire once again from somewhere inside the burning house, scattering the men who had ventured too near in their eagerness to claim the prisoners and sparking a crackle of return fire from the posse. And now I knew beyond doubt the identity of the rifleman.

I pointed the mules at the house and straddled one. Grasping its collar and reaching across to grip the other, I slipped down between them. It was a close fit and they didn't want me there; their restless whickers rumbled like growls from their ribs to mine. But nervous was good. I raised my feet, filled my lungs, emptied them in a high-pitched yell, and sank my teeth into the neck of the animal to my right. I tasted salt and blood. The mule brayed and they bolted, jolting my arms nearly out of their sockets. Hoofs drummed, the wind lashed my face, cold then hot as we neared the flames. Smoke stung my eyes but I didn't dare close them. If I calculated wrong they could wire me back to Montana in a Western Union envelope.

Through the water I saw the ruins of the porch come up and the instant before the mules turned to avoid a collision I let go. Splinters of pain shot up from the soles of my feet when I struck down. My knees buckled and I nearly fell in the terrified animals' path, but recovered myself on the run and bounded up and over the shambles of broken lumber, drawing the

Deane-Adams in midair and landing on my chest and elbows inside what used to be the front door.

For a second I lay there, floor-burned and slightly stunned, the revolver clamped in front of me between both palms. Then I rolled to the side. It was a time-tested tactic, but wasted. I was alone in the room.

It was a large parlor, and even through the blue haze I could see that it was elegantly furnished, with a Brussels carpet and overstuffed chairs and a massive old breakfront in the corner, eight feet tall and filled with blue china. Flames were snaffling at the printed wallpaper, blistering and blackening and peeling it as I watched and pouncing across the ceiling with a suckling roar. Orange coals the size of acorns dropped to the carpet and burned black holes on contact.

Ortiz had provided me with a description of the floor plan, and climbing to my feet I started toward the center of the house and the staircase leading to the tower. On the way there I spotted a corner of the carpet turned back. In the section of floor thus exposed I saw a square outline.

*With only a small trapdoor to defend, a man in that dark hole might withstand a siege of many months.*

Crouching on my heels to avoid silhouetting myself in the opening, I inserted my fingers in the crack between the boards and lifted.

Something scuffed the carpet behind me. I turned with the revolver. White light, brighter than any of the dynamite blasts, filled my skull. I felt myself tipping, threw out a hand to brace myself, and touched space. Warm moist blackness broke my fall.

\* \* \*

A train was champing at the platform, maintaining a head of steam.

The long hoarse chugs carried me back from wherever I'd been, to gray cold darkness and the beginning of an ache I knew from old experience would be with me for days and possibly weeks. Chiefly it was in my head, a living, breathing pain that bulged out of time with the uneven chugs and the smaller, sharper pains in my knees and elbows. The headache belonged to the blow that had taken me away from wherever I was now. I had acquired the others when I fell or was pushed to the hard smooth stony surface on which I lay. I placed a palm against it. Not stone; too even and, I sensed, not as hard. Not man-made, either; not even enough for that. Clay?

I turned onto my side. Through the murk I made out the faint gleam of light on glass, rows of curved glass objects stacked one on top of another, as on shelves. Jars? I began to know something.

Again I turned. I was on my back now, looking up at stripes of light some eight feet above me. I was disappointed in Ortiz. A good carpenter should be able to fit floorboards closer than that. As I was looking, a fall of glowing cinders showered down through the cracks and I threw a forearm across my eyes. The sparks stung my hand and face like hornets. The fire was still blazing. I couldn't have been out more than a few minutes.

The chugging continued, accompanied by a stream of dust and fresh cinders from above. Something blocked the light through several cracks. I remembered the big breakfront in the parlor then.

Someone was dragging it across the floor in the direction of the trapdoor. I thought I knew who.

The pain in my head bulged when I sat up, blinding me for a second. I reached up, touched the sticky mass behind my right ear, and snatched my hand away when a fresh bolt shot straight to the top of my skull. I put the hand down to push myself up and felt something I'd missed without even knowing it was gone. The cool solid patient shape of the Deane-Adams made me want to cry out. It must have dropped from my hand through the opening before Baronet could catch it. It was the only thing that had gone wrong with the trap he'd laid; but when a gambler's streak turns bad it doesn't stop.

I curled my fingers around the butt, rose to my knees, breathed, swallowed bile, and stood up. The basement did a slow Virginia reel and rocked to a standstill. I was ready to help move furniture.

A wooden ladder bolted to the stone wall led to the trapdoor. I holstered the pistol, climbed, and pushed with my hand. It didn't give. I went up another rung and leaned my shoulder against it. It was latched. I might have shot my way through. I might have cupped my hands around my mouth and shouted for freedom. Either way I would lose my only advantage. I climbed back down.

The man struggling with the breakfront paused to wheeze. I recognized Frank Baronet's voice. By now the ground floor would be full of smoke. Soon the boards would catch fire and collapse upon me, followed by the walls and roof. The trap had felt warm against my palm.

I drew the five-shot and looked up, calculating. Before my peacekeeping days I had spent a winter between roundups freighting iron stoves for a cartage company based in Saint Louis. My partner had a bad back and refused to pull against a weight, explaining that pushing was easier and not as likely to cause injury. His back wasn't nearly as bad as the sheriff's, not having a bullet in it. I waited until the breakfront began moving again, noting the angle by the pattern of falling dust and the shadow between the boards, and paced off the distance to the back. I pointed the revolver straight up and emptied the cylinder, spreading my shots in a loose pattern. Smoky light poked down through the holes.

There was a short space of silence. Then something thudded the floor, hard enough to shake loose a pound of old dirt and dry rot.

I reloaded from the loops on my belt, stepped beneath the trapdoor, and placed all five bullets in a tight group in one corner. The result was a ragged, fist-size hole. Once again I shook out the empty shells and replaced them with fresh cartridges, the last in my possession. I scaled the ladder, inserted my fingers in the hole, and pushed hard with the heel of my hand. The door gave a little. I mounted the last rung, placed my shoulder against the door and one foot against the nearest joist, and heaved upward. A moment's resistance, then the agonized shriek of tearing wood, and suddenly I was breathing the hot smoky air of freedom.

The walls were totally engulfed. Part of the ceiling was gone, having fallen into a pile of flaming debris that blocked the exit. The carpet, which Baronet had rucked back in order to move the breakfront, was burning, and threads of flame were blistering the veneer on that massive piece. Coughing and covering my nose and mouth with one hand, I stepped behind the breakfront. A smear of blood stained the floor and dribbled out into the hall leading to the back of the house. I followed it, gun in hand.

The drops grew faint and hard to distinguish against the brown leaf pattern on the hall runner. Then I came across a gout of it on the bottom step of the central staircase, as if he had paused there, hemorrhaging and supporting himself on the newel post. The trail continued up the stairs.

I climbed the first flight, flattened against the banister with the revolver pointed up the well. At the top was a landing and a steep flight of naked wooden steps ending in another trapdoor. This one hung open, releasing a flood of sunlight down the narrow passage from the open sentry tower atop the house. The blood trail led squarely up the middle.

My head throbbed. It seemed to be saying, *Not again.*

A second-floor hallway ran north and south from the landing. I peered in both directions. Through the roiling smoke it seemed to me I saw a faint smear where someone had mopped a fresh spill from the oiled floor in front of the first door south of the staircase.

Keeping the Deane-Adams in front of me, I backed toward the steep flight of steps and climbed them backward. They creaked loudly.

The door in the hallway flew open. I took an instant to identify Frank Baronet lunging across the threshold, his big Remington rolling-block pistol trained up the stairs. I fired twice into the thickest part of him. He stumbled, faltered, raised the pistol again. I fired again. He retreated into the room. The door closed.

I descended the steps. In the hallway I spread-eagled against the wall and stretched a hand toward the doorknob. The latch hadn't caught. The door opened at a touch. When no shots came from inside I pivoted around and through the opening, clasping the revolver in front of me at arm's length.

It was a bedroom, paneled in dark grainy oak and containing a bed with a six-foot carved headboard, a marble washstand, and a dropleaf secretary and matching cherrywood chair. Baronet sat in the chair with his back to the desk and his long legs splayed out in front of him, one arm curled over the back of the chair to prevent him from sliding. He was in his vest and shirtsleeves, just as he was when he dealt faro at the Orient, but his collar and cravat were missing and his white shirt was crosshatched with soot. His right hand rested in his lap with the single-shot pistol in it. A .45-70 Springfield rifle leaned in the corner next to the bed. It looked like the same one Ross Baronet had carried into the Apache Princess the night of the robbery.

" 'Satan's Sixgun.' " The sheriff laughed wheezily. "That piece doesn't even hold six."

His black hair, dank with sweat, hung in his eyes. His handlebars needed waxing. They drooped at the ends. The front of his person from the notch of his vest to the knees of his striped trousers was stained dark.

"Right now it's holding two," I said. "You should have shot me when you had the upper hand, instead of pistol-whipping me and dumping me into the cellar."

"We burn wife-stealers in this county."

It wasn't a subject for that part of the conversation. "You're all used up, Frank."

"I am not alone. There is no leaving this house now, for you or me. I designed it for dying in." A spasm shot through him, twisting his face into a rictus and tightening his grip on the back of the chair until his knuckles showed yellow. When it passed he was visibly weaker. Oxygen came hard. "I have got to ask why you carried it this far, Murdock. It wasn't because Ross tried to raid your place in San Sábado. Was it Colleen?"

"I didn't know about you and Colleen until a week ago."

"What, then? Did I use you so hard that day in Socorro City?"

"I've been used harder, and by worse than you," I said. "You should have let Dave and Vespa Spooner alone up in Lincoln. They made no difference to the war, and they got you killed."

He cast back. His brain was dying and thinking was a slow painful process. "That was months ago. What were the Spooners to you?"

"To me, nothing. Dave's father saved Judge Blackthorn's hide during the war with Mexico. The Judge asked me to come down here and pay his debt."

"I don't credit it. They were not worth all this bother. That's why I sent Ross to close their eyes."

That settled the point. I wondered why I felt no victory.

"Why did she shoot you?" I asked.

"The Spooner woman? She never. I don't believe I ever heard her speak."

"I mean Colleen Bower. Why did she shoot you?"

"What did she tell you?"

"She said you beat her up."

He smiled. It was as glassy-looking as his eyes. I doubted he could still see me. Seeing was becoming difficult for me as well. The air was thick with smoke and growing denser by the minute.

"Did you credit it?" he asked.

"I'm asking you."

The smile broadened. He raised the big pistol.

"Don't, Frank." I was still holding the Deane-Adams.

He tried to cock it. His thumb kept slipping off the hammer. He uncurled his other arm from the back of the chair to steady the gun while he tried again.

I cocked the revolver. "Don't."

He got the hammer back and locked. He raised the pistol. I shot him. He lost his brace and slid to the floor. Turned over on his side. I stepped forward and leaned down over him. "Why did she shoot you?"

"You still have a bullet." He pointed the Remington at me. I kicked it out of his grasp. The impact when it landed jarred loose the hammer. A bullet pierced the ceiling.

"Why did she shoot you, Frank?"

His lips were moving. I bent almost double, straining to hear the words. His mouth remained open when he stopped talking. His eyes did too.

When I failed to find a pulse anywhere on him I turned to the business of getting out. I got as far as the landing, where flames barred the stairs. I went back into the room, leaped over Baronet's body, pried at the window, found it painted shut, and kicked out the panes. Fire was chewing at the siding, but I climbed through the opening and stood on the sill, hanging on to the frame with one hand. I realized then I was still holding the Deane-Adams and jammed it into its holster. The drop was thirty feet to hard earth with nothing to slow me down. A pair of broken legs awaited me at the bottom, at the very least; a broken neck was more likely. Behind me the room was growing hot. I braced myself and pushed off.

Something swished past my ears and froze in front of my eyes, that familiar hang you looked for the instant before you leaned back with everything you had—but that was when you were on the other end. Instinctively I grabbed for it, but I wasn't fast enough and the loop closed under my arms and constricted my chest. My instinct then was to claw at the rope. Instead I hooked a foot inside the windowsill and turned to grasp the frame once again. As I did I looked up at the man on the other end of the rope. He was standing with his legs spread on the roof of the sentry tower, a thick silhouette against the sky in plain peasant dress without a hat.

"Miguel Axtaca?"

"This is my name," said the Aztec.

"How the hell did you get up there?"

"The same way we are going down." He fed me some slack for my descent and took another dally around the peak of the roof for his own.

# 24

THE BELL IN the church tower was swinging, calling the faithful of San Sábado to Mass. I was scrubbed and shaved and my scrapes and bruises had been seen to, but I wasn't dressed for worship, having packed everything but my trail clothes. On my way down the main street I encountered Rosario Ortiz coming out the front door of the Mare's Nest, where he took sourdough and coffee every morning with Eille Mac-Nutt in what was surely one of the most inexplicable friendships on record; what that pair had in common was anyone's guess. He had on his sombrero and his church suit, too tight in the chest and smelling of moth powder and cedar. He was one man who looked better in work clothes, be they stained overalls or cavalry kit and weapons. When he saw me he inclined his head.

"*Buenos días, Señor* Murdock. It is a fine morning to greet the Lord, is it not?"

"I suppose. I'll be glad enough to get up in the Bitterroots and greet some snow. I have had my fill of sunshine and adobe."

"You are leaving today?"

"I should have left last week, but I'm punishing Judge Blackthorne. His reply when I wired him about what happened at the Baronet ranch was less than polite."

"I think I see. He has guilt that the burden of justice fell to you, who had no personal stake in the matter, instead of to him."

"Maybe," I said. "If I live to be forty-one I'll never know what goes on under his hat."

"What do you intend to do with your interest in the Apache Princess?"

"That's what I'm on my way to discuss with Mrs. Bower." I stuck out my hand. "*Vaya con dios,* Marshal. I am coming away with that much Spanish at least."

He took it. For a moment he seemed on the edge of saying something. Then he ducked his head again and hastened across the street to join the crowd drifting toward the church. We were as ill at ease in each other's company as a man and woman who had become lovers for one night, only to awaken the next morning to find they had nothing in common but the passion of the moment. I never saw or heard from him again. If he's dead I hope he made it to heaven despite his convictions to the contrary.

At the alley I paused to raise my hat to a gaggle of widows hauling a train of dust with their black hems. They looked neither left nor right, turning the corner in a body on their way to church; identical in their weeds, anonymous behind their veils, and as formi-

dable after their fashion as the combined and righ-
teous might of the riders of the Diamond Horn and
the Slash W, who had parted company upon deliver-
ing their prisoners to Lew Wallace in Santa Fe. By
now they would have reverted to their old habits,
rustling each other's cattle and trading shots across
the oldest and bloodiest border in the western hemi-
sphere. My last sight of Miguel Axtaca, after he had
risked his life to save mine at the Baronet spread, had
been of his broad unadorned back riding south between Francisco and Carlos at the head of Don
Segundo's loyal band of vaqueros. His kind is gone
now, if indeed it ever existed outside the early Spanish accounts of the Mexican conquest; even the dust
of their bones has settled over the caves and deserts of
Chihuahua and Sonora, indistinguishable from the
sand. Don Segundo del Guerrero is no less dead now,
his ranch divided, the lions he loved to hunt gone the
way of the Aztec and the Spanish grandee. We will
not see their autocratic like.

John Whiteside died in Cuba. Against the advice
of his friends, including Theodore Roosevelt, he had
insisted at the age of seventy-four upon leading his
own regiment of hand-picked cowboys into battle
with the Spaniards, only to succumb to yellow fever
in the stinking hold of a troopship in Havana Harbor
without ever having set foot on the island. His body
was brought back to New Mexico by some of his men
for burial. You can't miss the monument. It's the tall-
est thing in Socorro County west of Chupader Mesa.

Judge Blackthorne, in forced retirement at the
time and diverting his still-prodigious energies into
articles for *Galaxy* and *Harper's Weekly*, wrote that the

"Cuban debacle" may yet justify its expense by providing a dumping ground for "apoplectic grandfathers who have read Homer and taken him too much to heart." Then he, too, in excellent health and at the peak of his mental abilities, expired. A number of sanguinary accounts of his years on the bench were published in the years afterward, running about half for and half against. History hasn't yet decided what to make of him, and neither, by God, have I.

Colleen Bower answered the door at *Señora* Castillo's boardinghouse wearing a plain black dress cinched cruelly at the waist and covering everything from just below her chin to the shiny caps of her patent-leather shoes. Her hair was pinned up in back and she wore no paint, the first time I had seen her that way at that hour of the morning. She looked neither young nor old. *Timeless* was the word that came to mind. I removed my hat.

"I haven't much time, Page. I am late for church as it is."

"I won't keep you long. I just came to say goodbye. Where is the old witch?"

"She went on ahead. You're really leaving?" She closed the door behind me and led the way into the Victorian/Porfiristan parlor. We remained standing, facing each other across the earthen floor.

I nodded. "I'm taking the short route by way of El Paso and catching the train from there. General Crook has Geronimo cornered in Arizona, so it should be safe."

"What about the Princess?"

"I'm selling out my third for what I paid. If you're interested, you can wire the money to Judge Blackthorne at the federal courthouse in Helena. It was his money to begin with. If you like you can advertise that for a little while you were partners with the Iron Jurist."

"I think I won't. It would only frighten away business. As it happens, however, I am interested. Eille MacNutt has asked to buy in. I was planning to discuss it with you, but I guess now I won't have to."

"So that's what you talked about during those long buggy rides," I said. "I wondered."

"He has a sound head for business, whatever else you may think of him. With the sheriff dead and county politics in a tangle, Wallace is considering a declaration of martial law. It will be an excellent time to acquire property, as the values are sure to be depressed. When the order is lifted and the immigrants start streaming in, the scramble will be on for every available acre. Eille has the capital. I am the draw. Are you sure you don't want to stay? There will be more than money enough for three."

"I'd just waste it on food and shelter." I reached inside my hat. "Eille now, is it?"

"You have a filthy mind, Page. Perhaps law work is best for you after all."

I gave her the slip of paper I'd removed from the sweatband. "That's the address of Junior Harper's mother in Chicago. I found it in his wallet. You can send his share of the profits to her."

"Does she know?"

"Yes. I wired her from Socorro City and made arrangements to ship his body north. I'm sure if you offer to buy out his interest she'll go along. She is no saloonkeeper."

She folded the paper and tucked it inside her sleeve. "I'm sorry about Junior, Page."

"Are you?"

"Of course. I liked Junior. If it were not for him—"

"If it weren't for him you'd still be married to Frank Baronet and required by law to share your property with him. As his widow you're free and clear, with the added advantage of a little gentlemanly sympathy on the part of the men who challenge your board. That's why you're dressed in black. You wore the ring Baronet gave you to keep them at arm's length. Now you wear mourning to keep them off guard. And you owe it all to Junior."

"I told you he was drunk! He asked me to marry him, and when he found out Frank was my husband he went crazy. I tried to stop him."

"Did you tell him Frank beat you?"

"He wanted to know why I left. I told him the truth."

"You told him what you told me, that you shot Frank out of fear and pain and ran away because you thought you'd killed him. Junior was a romantic. The story made him angry and filled his head with notions of chivalry. He was drunk, but he sobered up on the trail. He'd have turned back then if you hadn't mentioned that beating.

"But he was only part of it," I went on. "You knew Junior was no match for the sheriff and Jubilo both. You sent him to his death, knowing I'd go after his killers. The beating story worked as well with me as it had with Junior, putting just the right edge on it.

Hell, you had an army on your side. It was one hand you couldn't lose."

"You saw the scar."

"You got it in a fight with a jealous whore."

Her skin went transparent. I could see the network of bones and muscles in her face. "Did Frank tell you that?" Her voice was metallic.

"Jubilo did. Frank told me why you shot him."

She said nothing.

"They were his very last words," I said. " 'I don't go partners with anyone.' Quite an epitaph."

"It doesn't prove anything."

"There's nothing to prove. The only crime you committed was shooting a sheriff in the back, and he's dead by my hand. The only crime anyone can arrest you for in this life, that is. If I were you, I'd look out for Marshal Ortiz in the next. He thinks he's damned too, and all he did was put a bullet in his wife's brain when she begged him to."

"I was his draw."

I barely heard her. I asked her to repeat it.

She did. Her voice rose. "I drew his customers to the Orient. There are eleven saloons in Socorro City, and a faro table in each one. Why did they come there if not to play cards with a pretty woman? I herded them in, I fleeced them, and I sent them back out grinning to earn more wages so they could come back. I thought when I married Frank he would deal me in for half. That was my mistake; I should have made certain. He laughed when I asked him about it. Laughed in my face and showed me his back."

"Never a wise choice where you're concerned."

She tried to claw my face. I caught her wrists and forced them down to her sides. She struggled fiercely—there was pure sinew under the slender sheathing of her arms and legs, and she was filled with hate—then stopped. I watched her drawing composure from deep inside, like a glacier generating a fresh layer of ice to heal a scar. It would be the same way she handled a bad turn of cards. After a minute I let go. She smiled as she did when a player approached her table and turned toward the door.

"I wish you'd reconsider your decision to leave." She lifted a small black felt hat from the ledge of the coatrack, an elaborate piece in carved mahogany complete with a built-in umbrella stand and a mirror framed in giltwood, standing next to the plain plank door. If *Señora* Castillo's theories on decorating ever caught on back East, there would be no stopping them. "How many years can a man have to wear the badge, and what does he have when he is through? You are already an old man in your work."

"I still prefer the odds."

She fixed the hat to her hair with a pin long enough to picket a horse and gathered up her reticule. The pocket pistol inside made it hang crooked when she slid the loop over her wrist. "It's a pity. I like you, Page. We could have enjoyed each other."

"You liked Junior."

She glared briefly at my reflection in the mirror. Then she lowered her veil over an expression of trackless purity and went out to join the other widows.

Estleman, Loren D.
  City of widows

F-C

| | DATE DUE | | |
|---|---|---|---|
| | | | |
| | | | |
| | | | |
| | | | |
| | | | |
| | | | |
| | | | |
| | | | |
| | | | |
| | | | |
| | | | |
| | | | |

5|94